VINTAGE

INTERNATIONAL

Erich Hackl

AURORA'S MOTIVE

Translated from the German by Edna McCown

Vintage International
Vintage Books
A Division of Random House, Inc.
New York

FIRST VINTAGE INTERNATIONAL EDITION, FEBRUARY 1990

Library of Congress Cataloging-in-Publication Data
Hackl, Erich.
    [Auroras Anlass. English]
    Aurora's motives / Erich Hackl ; translated from the German by Edna McCown. —1st Vintage international ed.
        p.   cm.—(Vintage international)
    Translation of: Aurora Anlass.
    "First published in the United States by Alfred A. Knopf, Inc., in New York, in 1988"—T.p. verso
    ISBN 0-679-72435-4 : $7.95
    1. Rodríguez, Aurora, 1890–   —Fiction.   2. Hildegart, pseud.—Fiction.   I. Title
PT2668.A2717A9513   1990
833'.914—dc20   89-40085
                                          CIP

Manufactured in the United States of America
10 9 8 7 6 5 4 3 2 1

It is a terrible thing to do
to unusual people, to drive
them so deeply into themselves
that each reemergence is a
volcanic explosion.

GUNTRAM VESPER,
North of Love and South of Hate

AURORA'S MOTIVE

1

One day Aurora Rodríguez was compelled to kill her daughter. She went into her bedroom and from the night table took out a pistol that she had bought months before to protect Hildegart's life, should that be necessary. She loaded the weapon, released the safety catch, and entered her daughter's room without hesitation. She closed the door behind her softly, fumbled in the dark for the lamp standing on a low table piled high with books and newspapers near the bed, then fired four shots. According to the opinion later given by a forensic specialist, the first two slugs were fatal, having penetrated Hildegart's heart; the second two were fired at such close range that the skin of the right temple was burned and a strand of her daughter's brown curly hair was singed. Before leaving the room, Aurora turned out the light and raised the jalousies from in front of the windows. Then she stuck the pistol in her handbag, got dressed, and left the apartment.

On the steps she met the maidservant, Julia Sanz,

who had left the building a half hour before to walk her mistresses' dogs. Aurora Rodríguez told the woman that she wouldn't be back and that she, Julia, should take the dogs that morning to Señora Carbayo Orenga to care for, as had been arranged several days before. Julia Sanz attached no further meaning to her remark, as she assumed that Aurora Rodríguez was taking a trip to Mallorca together with her daughter, as had been discussed often in the last few days. She merely asked if the neighbor had already received the money for the care of the animals (four pesetas per day). Aurora Rodríguez affirmed this and petted the dogs before she went on. When Julia Sanz opened the apartment door, she immediately noticed the strong odor of gunpowder.

Aurora Rodríguez proceeded without further ado to the office of a lawyer she knew well, to whom she confessed her deed. The dumbfounded attorney, a prominent Radical Socialist politician who was scheduled to assume the office of Minister of Justice a few months later, accompanied her at her wish to the Palace of Justice, where Aurora Rodríguez presented herself to the authorities.

Despite certain doubts concerning the veracity of the confession—doubts fed by the widespread knowledge of the close and harmonic relationship between Aurora and her daughter Hildegart—the magistrate and the forensic pathologist on duty went to the woman's apartment. There they met two policemen who had been summoned by the distressed maid, who could not stop sobbing.

Aurora Rodríguez, who was taken to the women's prison at Noviciado in northwestern Madrid after being

5

interrogated, was the daughter of Pilar Carballeira, who had been trained as a teacher, but had never worked in her profession. Aurora's mother, who had never shown her any tenderness, as she testified in court, had died twenty-nine years before, after which Aurora Rodríguez was the only one of four siblings to remain at home. She spent the next three years in the company of her father, whose death deprived her of her closest confidant.

Her father, an attorney and court procurator, had been well-respected in El Ferrol, a major harbor city of northwestern Spain, although his neighbors did not deny that his opinions were a bit extreme. At the social gatherings, the *tertulias*, that Anselmo Rodríguez attended with friends and acquaintances at the municipal club, he was reported to have expressed a great appreciation for the people of the former Spanish colonies of Central and South America. Also, his opinions on the naval war with the United States were in no way shared by the majority of the population, especially not by its city fathers and prominent citizens. Though he considered the enemy to be a danger not only to national security but to the human race in general, he nonetheless made it known that his sympathies lay, not with the Spanish naval forces, but with the great freedom fighters, Maceo and Rizal. Criticized by his companions for a lack of patriotism, he countered that all the truly great men of history, regardless of origin, had always placed freedom above petty national disputes.

Besides which, I don't understand why national interests are defended so vehemently here in Galicia, when this part of the country is one of the poorest and most exploited. And it is precisely the sons of this region, peasants and fishermen, who serve their fatherland as cannon fodder for the enemy.

The other men said nothing to this, and Anselmo Rodríguez also fell silent. He had the feeling that he had ventured into an area where he should proceed with caution.

In 1898, following the loss of the overseas colonies of Cuba and the Philippines, eight-year-old Aurora was allowed to accompany her father to the piers in El Ferrol where the defeated Spanish fleet had put in. She stood before the high ships' walls, mute and fearful, and it was strange to her to see Anselmo Rodríguez raise his hat to the hollow-cheeked, ragged figures on board. Other than the two of them, and women dressed in black, peasant women from the hinterland who hoped against hope to recognize one of their sons, no one had come to greet those returning home.

Ingratitude, said her father, is the way of the world. Aurora should mark this day well; she would live to see a time, or so he hoped, when the humbled would receive justice. A time when the bankers, who had gotten rich on this war, the bishops, who had blessed these ships, and the admirals, who had commanded the fleet from the safety of Madrid, would be called to account.

Aurora was drawn to her father. By renouncing his role as head of the household, Anselmo Rodríguez acquired the quiet time he needed at the end of each workday to contemplate his ideals concerning better conditions in his country. Aurora's mother, Pilar Carballeira, was intolerant, hard, ill-humored. She tried with great effort to lead a life modeled on that of other families, those of doctors, high officers, landowners.

She insisted that her four children go to church on Sundays, engaged servants to do things she herself had enjoyed doing before, forbade her two daughters, Aurora and Josefa, who was ten years older, to jump and run, even as small children, and allowed only her last-born, a boy, to attend school, and that only because a respected private institution had opened in the town. The other children were educated at home by a distant relative whose parents had become impoverished following a failed business speculation. But this young woman's knowledge and pedagogical skills were rather wanting, on top of which she did not dare to put an end once and for all to the mischievous pranks of the two oldest children. Aurora Rodríguez learned from her what every well-educated young lady learned: reading, writing, basic arithmetic, knitting, how to play the piano, and a few ghastly scraps of French.

One day a maidservant whom Aurora trusted greatly took the little girl home with her, to her village. It was during the Festival of San Pedro, patron saint of the village, and there was dancing on the plaza under garlands of multicolored pennants. The servant girl knew that her fiancé was in the crowd. So she asked her mother to pay special attention to Aurora for a while. Then she went to the dance. Her mother, following her request, attempted to entertain Aurora, who was glancing furtively about the single room of the house. Yet the child had a hard time understanding her; she was unfamiliar with Gallego, considered as a dialect at home. She was frightened by the other children's curiosity about her. And the unaccustomed poverty of her surroundings, the straw sacks, the clay floor, and the chickens strutting about on it were so strange to her that she soon insisted that she be allowed to go to the dance and watch the woman's daughter.

After Aurora had been told how to get there, she went to the village plaza. But, try as she could, she couldn't make out the girl among the dancers. Just as she turned to run back to the house, near tears, she glimpsed a couple on the corner, kissing passionately. Only when the man gave the servant girl a nudge did she notice Aurora. She blushed, disengaged herself from his embrace, and took the child by the hand.

At home over dinner, Aurora Rodríguez innocently told about the dance and the kiss in the village. Her older brother and sister giggled, her father wasn't listening, as usual. But Señora Carballeira dismissed the girl that same night.

Another time, when Aurora's older brother began prowling about the servants' quarters and hiding under the stairs to look up their skirts, her mother talked her husband into offering the kitchen maid money to initiate the young man into the practices of love. The girl, who was known to have already had several lovers, and who reassured them that she was healthy, brought in her parents for consultation. They agreed, on condition that Anselmo Rodríguez find work on a freighter to Cuba for one of their sons, who had to emigrate to America because their property barely served to support their first-born son. Aurora's father went one step further and procured for the girl a license to sell tobacco in the court of law where he appeared daily. The girl's parents thanked him profusely. He extricated himself from their handshakes in embarrassment. The incident was for him proof of his country's decadence and agony. In his library, he wrote in his diary: The suffering of the lower classes is unbearable. Their situation can be changed only by blind rage, violence, blood, and fire. But that doesn't occur to them, because all of their strength is directed toward naked survival, because they are in the clutches of the false morality of those who are better off than they, and because they seek personal advantage without recognizing that that even further entangles them in their misery. The privileged live in comfort. We can see that everything is coming apart, but we're afraid of change. We are dissatisfied, but we are cowards.

Then he buried himself in the *Latin World Review* whose latest issue had just arrived. In an essay by a certain Valentí Almirall, obviously a Catalonian, he found a passage that seemed to him to capture Spain's tragedy. *This nation lives in total negation, in a true orgy of negative ideas. Ask Spaniards if they are monarchists and they will reply in the negative. Then ask them if they are republicans. They will answer that in the negative also. What are they, then? They don't know. They are content to reject everything. The old fatalism has taken over anew. The peasant ekes out his existence without in the least attempting to shake off ignorance, monotonous routine, poverty. The city dweller lives on the peasant, who can barely scratch out a survival on the land. Progress has not yet reached us. Spiritual life has ceased to exist.*

In eluding her mother, whose rules seemed erratic and unfair to her, Aurora landed in her father's library. Unlike her siblings, she was not intimidated by the dark spines of the books, nor by the quiet of the high, narrow room. In addition, Anselmo Rodríguez's study, where he dispensed legal advice in the afternoons, was separated from the library only by double doors. Owing to the discussions in the adjoining room, she never felt lonely. But she was nevertheless alone.

One day, when Aurora must have been seven years old, her father received a lady. Though his daughter was busy dressing and undressing a doll, she was soon listening attentively to the woman's excited voice.

Anselmo Rodríguez, who knew the woman's husband, a Señor Balboa, owner of the city's largest hardware store, at first believed this to be a private visit. But the woman's somber mien told him that she had not come to issue an invitation, or in preparation for the annual bazaar of the Christian Charity, of which Señora Balboa was head. He agreed to her request that he tell no one, not even his wife, of the subject of their talk, citing his practice of professional confidentiality.

The woman hesitated before saying softly, but loud enough for the little girl in the next room to hear, that she had come to begin divorce proceedings against her husband. The lawyer was at first too surprised to answer. The woman hurried to add that her decision was final. Of all the lawyers in the city, she had the greatest trust in Anselmo Rodríguez, and therefore wished to engage him in the carrying out of the necessary steps.

Aurora's father asked if she was aware of the consequences of her decision. Señora Balboa nodded, repeating that she could not be shaken in her resolution, which she had come to after careful consideration. She was also aware of the material consequences, but did not see them as an obstacle, as her share of her parents' inheritance would guarantee her and her daughter an adequate subsistence. Anselmo Rodríguez asked on what grounds she based the dissolution of her marriage. When the woman paused, he said that he wasn't asking her this question out of curiosity. Without knowing the cause, he could not be of help to her.

Señora Balboa now began to cry; she admitted, sobbing, that she had lost all feelings of affection for her husband. She felt fear, revulsion, and hate each time he approached her. She was overcome by disgust when he lay on top of her. She increasingly felt like an object to be taken whenever her husband wished, and to be pushed away when she had done her duty. After a while, Anselmo Rodríguez asked if there were any other reasons, more concrete ones.

Isn't that enough?

Aurora's father assured her that he understood her fully, but pointed out that the current divorce laws would not admit such motives. Señora Balboa must reckon with the fact that she would be considered the guilty party if she brought this charge before the court.

It doesn't matter, the woman replied, if it results in a divorce!

Aurora's father asked if she had also considered her child. He stood up, took a book from a bookcase and opened it. The civil law established in 1889 did not recognize such doubtlessly honorable arguments. Article 73: If the divorce was granted, it would have the following results: First, the couple would be separated from bed and board. Second, any offspring of the marriage would remain under the authority and care of the innocent party.

The lawyer snapped the book shut: That is the law. In order to prevent the woman from once again breaking into tears, he quickly added that of course he did not know if her husband attached any value to retaining custody of their child. If he did not, it might be possible to find a satisfactory solution, such as, in the event that her husband relinquished custody, another person's being appointed guardian, someone who was close to Señora Balboa and who would not be a hindrance to her in bringing up her daughter. But the woman waved away this suggestion. Her decision to seek Señor Rodríguez's counsel had not been a hasty one. It had been preceded by countless arguments, at the end of which her husband had announced to her scornfully that she could file for divorce if she liked, but in that case, he would insist on custody of their child. If only to hurt his wife.

As Aurora pressed her doll close to herself in the adjoining room, her father regretfully shrugged his shoulders. Señora Balboa stood up and shook his hand. I'm sorry, he said. What will you do?

Suffer hell. I will not give up Rosa.

When Anselmo Rodríguez entered his library later, his daughter still sat with her doll in her arms. That's a pretty doll, he said. What's her name?

Rosa, Aurora said. And she belongs only to me.

2

An unstable, helpless creature, Hildegart would write, *who constantly conforms to the image that society has of her, who shrinks from acknowledging her own secret desires, who never talks openly with men, always lowers her eyes, allows herself to be led around by the nose—that is the Spanishwoman. With honorable exceptions, she possesses a monstrous sexual appetite. In this, she is related neither to the Englishwoman, who long retains her innocence, nor to the precocious Frenchwoman. The Spanishwoman's sexual drive can be traced back to the abstinence that has been forced upon her for centuries. She is the victim of religious ideas of morality that have led her to sense vulgarity where there is only science, and pornography where there is only truth and nature.* In Aurora's later judgment, her sister, Josefa, had coarse, asymmetrical features that, together, projected a sensuality and attracted men. Even as a child she treated the maids in an extremely insulting manner, nor did she balk at blaming her sister for her own wicked deeds. If, at the command of Señora Carballeira, one of the servants forbade snacks between meals, or reported her impudent behavior to her mother, she took revenge.

When Aurora was four years old, Josefa ordered her to hide a ring in a maid's closet, a ring that Josefa had taken from her mother's jewelry box. The child did as she was told, without exactly understanding what she was doing. Señora Carballeira, who always thought she was being cheated by the domestic help, missed the piece of jewelry on the same day. Josefa, who had sworn her sister to secrecy, steered suspicion to the maid, in whose closet the ring was indeed found. The young woman's protests helped little. She was driven out of the house; Aurora's mother insisted on reporting the alleged theft to the police. Only after several days did Aurora dare to tell her father the truth. But who believes a little girl's confused stories? At any rate, Anselmo Rodríguez withdrew the charge.

The private governess was a frequent victim of the children's pranks. Isabel Monteiro, a skinny, oldish spinster had waited for years for a marriageable man, to no avail. She seldom spoke and was content when the Rodríguez children occupied themselves quietly and left her time during instruction hours to read long-winded novels in which chivalrous men courted virtuous Christian women. Josefa and Aurora's older brother amused themselves in gluing the leaves of the book together or ripping out the last pages, so that the impatient reader was deprived of the happy ending of quietly burning passions. As Josefa got older, she enjoyed embarrassing Señorita Monteiro with her questions on the propagation of the human race. Or she pointedly asked what those two dogs were doing, the ones in the unusual

position that she had observed yesterday. At this the
woman would turn away, carrying on about the birds and
bees, blush at the children's laughter, and put off the
explanation to another day.

Once, as Aurora was playing in the garden, she heard
a sound coming from a secluded room in a side wing of
the house. She stood on her tiptoes and saw her sister,
naked down to her stockings, her legs spread and
wrapped around a man's bare back. Both were breathing
heavily, then her sister's panting became a whimper, she
tossed her head from one side to the other, the man
above her with a bald spot on his head, his shoulders
covered with hair.

Aurora wanted to turn away, to run away, *disgusted*,
as she confessed to the High Court, but her legs
wouldn't obey. She saw how the man raised himself and
wiped his member with a handkerchief, how Josefa, still
lying on her back, stretched out her legs, put one hand
under her head, and observed the naked man indiffer-
ently, even mockingly, it appeared to the child who
stood there staring in spite of the danger of being discovered, and even though the balls of her feet hurt.

Long after Josefa no longer took instruction from Señorita Monteiro, there occurred an inexplicable change
in her physical condition. She began to suffer from
spells of dizziness, of queasiness, she threw up every
morning at the sight of her favorite food. Aurora's sister
also became subject to mood changes. She was mostly
despondent, but then suddenly happy for no reason at
all; in an outburst of warmth she would throw her arms
around Aurora, who up until that time had never known
such tenderness.

The two sisters shared a room, and when her sister's

indisposition first set in, Aurora wanted to inform her parents. But Josefa entreated her to say nothing. Her condition was due to the sudden growth of her limbs and the internal changes that young women frequently experienced and was therefore no cause for alarm; it would take care of itself. She didn't want to upset her parents when there was nothing really wrong.

So Aurora kept quiet, even when she noticed several weeks later that her sister's face and legs were swollen and Josefa was putting on weight, despite the obvious fact that she was eating less. Even though she corseted herself tightly each morning, Josefa could soon no longer hide her condition. One day she fainted at lunch. After she had been taken quickly to the divan in the salon and her clothes loosened, her predicament became clear to her parents. Aurora was sent to her room, and from there she heard her mother's cries and the sound of the slaps with which Señora Carballeira called Josefa back to consciousness. It was also with slaps that the future grandmother got out of Josefa the name of the man she had slept with. As he, contrary to her fears, was a single man of social standing, it was possible to find a solution that would preserve the family's honor.

This was all rather unimportant to Anselmo Rodríguez, who more and more retreated to his library, rarely took on cases, and performed only what was absolutely necessary at court. His wife's agitation seemed out of proportion in view of the general state of the world and its morals. Anyway, there was enough money to feed one more mouth.

José Arriola, the man who had impregnated Josefa, was a textile merchant who had returned a few years before from America, where he had made his fortune. He paid the family a formal visit several days later. He didn't appear particularly remorseful, which secretly pleased Aurora's father, but he did brag about his wealth, which, as Anselmo Rodríguez confided to his younger daughter, had been made at the cost of Indians and Negroes. There was nothing standing in the way of his marriage to Josefa; but his business, which took him here and there at present, would make it impossible for him to lead a quiet family life until his retirement. It was agreed that the child would be left with its grand-parents; Josefa, who until the end of her pregnancy never came to terms with her role as mother, wanted to share Arriola's adventurous life. Señora Carballeira was not opposed to this, as it would prevent the couple, of disparate ages and experience, from drifting apart.

Josefa bore a healthy boy and, scarcely up from childbed, packed her bag and followed her husband. The child, who was named for his father, was suckled by a wet nurse.

As his grandmother paid little attention to him, he soon sought the favor of his aunt, who returned his af-fection. Aurora would carry the child for hours on walks, protect him from the adults' irritability and dis-cord, and sing him to sleep at night. If Pepito, as she affectionately called him, was irritated or sad, she would play lullabies for him on her mother's piano, short songs composed especially for children. At first she did this only now and again, but it soon became a daily custom that neither of them wished to miss. Pepito sat on Aurora's lap during the concerts, still, intent, obviously sunk in the sound of the notes.

They seldom heard from his mother. Occasionally, small gifts would arrive by mail, *for my little monkey, my heart, our good little boy:* brightly painted wooden horses with or without wagons, a trumpet, tin soldiers. And there would be colored postcards with the royal palace in Madrid, the Giralda in Seville, Barcelona's Ramblas. On the back were hastily-written greetings, *Imagine, Joselito, yesterday I saw the king, we received an invitation from the Count of Alba, tomorrow we travel to Paris. Be good and obey your dear grandparents.* Pepito was not impressed by this attention; the toys soon lay forgotten in some corner; the postcards were of interest only as long as Aurora told him stories about the cities they depicted.

Aurora found the material for these stories in her father's books, which she devoured indiscriminately, at first. With the exception of short excursions to surrounding villages, a few trips to La Coruña, where Pilar Carballeira updated her wardrobe, and the annual stay at the family's summer house eighteen miles inland, the first twenty-four years of her life were spent in El Ferrol. She was eager to find out what was going on in the world, and when she was permitted to accompany her father to his club, she hung onto his words as he recalled the deeds of those who had fought for freedom, and cautiously, but constantly, spoke of the social problems that would be resolved only through a totally new social order.

In his circle of notaries, physicians, and garrison officers, no one could imagine how this quaint bird, Rodríguez, was going to abolish evil from the world.

Dear colleague, you are only giving support to those murderous thugs in Andalusia.

No, no, I do not exalt violence.

Exactly. It's not for everyone. And besides our life is no bed of roses.

Aurora's father disputed that. We have it good. We have more than we deserve. And whom do we have to thank for that? The ignorance of the common people, who procreate all too freely because they don't know the simplest rules of nature. Because they are stupid. And because they own so little land, hardly enough to sustain themselves, the poor are forced to engage in work that is so inadequately rewarded that they have the choice of either scraping along or turning to murder in order to get what is being denied them.

A state prosecutor who was also sitting at the table, protested against this one-sided, *demagogic* rationalization of crime. You're using that to excuse every act of violence.

Anselmo Rodríguez would not be put off. During the course of their lives these poor creatures, who, after all, make up eighty percent of our population, and even more here in Galicia, will have no chance to acquire knowledge. The Church shields them from it and feeds them superstition. So they continue to multiply like rabbits and struggle for their children's daily bread, and are, of course, unable to educate themselves.

What could change that?

At the very least, a policy of population control that would include sexual education and encourage abstinence, which, in the beginning, might need to be instituted by force. Wealth would be better distributed if there were fewer poor people.

That seemed clear. The men proceeded to the day's order of business and discussed curious legal cases, the

Minister of the Army's recent edicts, and strides made in medicine. In closing, they made fun of the parish priest's latest sermon; though they were all freethinkers, none of them missed high mass.

Anselmo Rodríguez returned in a good mood from a trip to the south, occasioned by a protracted lawsuit among siblings. He had to admit that his clients' case looked even more complicated than he had thought before his trip, and he had been unable to inspect several documents that he hoped to procure. But, as he told his daughter, during his trip east of Seville he had by accident come across an estate that was being communally farmed and run by a group of day laborers since the death of the prior owner.

Imagine, said Aurora's father, a voluntary coalition of simple folk, thirty men and their families, made possible only through the altruism of the former proprietor, who died of a stroke. And it offers a decent living, despite the animosity of the neighboring large landowners, who send their peons at night to lay waste the fields, forcing the community to greater vigilance. In the long run, of course, success can be guaranteed only by independence through self-sufficiency, larger units, that is, three hundred families on four thousand hectares of fertile soil, which would ensure a communal agronomy. Clothing would also have to be provided; and they would have to keep animals, cattle, pigs, and sheep, whose wool would protect them from the cold. Whether farmer, cobbler, blacksmith, cartwright, or baker—all would make use of their abilities and talents. It would not be necessary to pay anyone. Everything would rest on voluntarism. Money would be done away with. Every

decision would be made consensually. There would be
no subordination, no coercion or submission.

And the women? Aurora asked. And the children?

He wasn't too concerned about the children. They
would grow up autonomous in such a collective environment, could develop their talents in peace. Attributes
of the present society, such as envy, selfishness, and
avarice, would be a burden to communal life at first.
But the next generation would be free of that. Yes, it
would be easier for the children to comprehend this new
form of communal life as the solely natural one. They
would become familiar from childhood on with the various work procedures in the workshops, in the fields and
forests. They would learn at play how to spin, milk,
construct wagon wheels, dig ditches, shear sheep, cul-
tivate the land and harvest the crops. Whoever wanted
to become a doctor would learn everything about the
healing power of herbs, would learn how to set broken
bones, and would attend births.

But the servants!

There would be no servants. Neither master nor
underling. And no privileges, including those of man
over woman. Heavy physical work would have to be
done by the men. On the other hand, women were much
better suited for activities that required dexterity and
patience. All laws that limited the lives of women would
be abolished. A husband would not be permitted to take
liberties with his wife; she could not be put at his disposal. Anyway, it should be considered whether such a
way of life called for marriage at all.

But why was he telling her all of this?

It is useless. This country is ruined from the ground

up. No one can imagine a situation different from the present one. Neither the rich, because they don't want to work, nor the poor, because they have never learned to think. Or because they hope to become rich one day themselves. Neither the men, because they rule the women, nor the women, because they accept their role, and punish with scorn and contempt anyone among them who fights it. Yes, the women are hyenas, and if nothing changes in Spain, then it will be because the priests have won the women over to their side.

Aurora Rodríguez had a hard time accepting the idea that she belonged to the sex that was held in such low esteem by her father. She was forbidden to do many things that were permitted her brothers. She was stuck in uncomfortable clothes that took a long time to put on in the morning, and had to learn to soften her voice and never to look a man in the eyes. From twelve years of age on she was no longer allowed to go out on the street by herself. It was a source of constant irritation to Señora Carballeira that her father took her with him now and then to his club.

Aurora was shocked when she first began menstruating at fourteen. Unlike her sister, however, she didn't think she was bleeding to death. She knew what it was about from reading the books on medical advice in her father's library. But she saw herself now as a woman, a second-class citizen, and was convinced that much in life would be withheld from her. To change her life in such a manner that *all* life was changed—that appeared almost hopeless to her.

On top of this, she lost Pepito, whom she had long considered her own. In her hands, her sister's son had become a *Wunderkind,* according to the newspapers, Mozart reincarnate.

It had all started with a little piece Aurora Rodríguez was playing on the piano, her three-year-old nephew on her lap. Suddenly, in the middle of the piece, Pepito pushed his aunt's hands away and played the notes himself, *more purely, better, than I had ever done.* Aurora was delighted. She called the family together, her father, who was sitting in his study, her mother, who was instructing a chambermaid in the use of a feather duster, and her younger brother. They all stood beside the piano and marveled at the small child's musical gift (he was still wetting his bed at night), *my work.*

Two months later Pepito gave his first concert, in a circle of friends and acquaintances, and then one in the theater in El Ferrol. A better teacher was hired; Aurora was no longer needed. Then they heard from Josefa, *my little monkey;* suddenly there was room for the child in the Arriola family, even if Pepito kicked and screamed when they came to get him.

What could be done for a genius in this forgotten corner of the country, among uneducated provincials? There was not one teacher left in the entire town who believed himself capable of preparing the boy further. In Madrid, his parents promised, only the best music instructors would be considered; there was also a wealth of artistic offerings—a cosmopolitan city, after all.

And, in fact, the Rodríguez family received frequent reports from the capital, enthusiastic letters from Josefa with newspaper clippings attached. *Pepe Arriola conquers Madrid,* concerts in the Ateneo, in the royal palace, in the Teatro Real. Aurora sought in vain for evidence, signs, that her nephew had not forgotten her. Then the Arriolas moved to Paris, *José Arriola, the Spanish Wunderkind. A four-year-old pianist conquers Europe.*

Later, the letters got shorter, the newspaper reports briefer—from the provinces now, less and less from the larger regional press, the tone sharper or bored. Then nothing more was heard from her nephew. His grandparents didn't live long enough to hear of his descent to playing piano in a bar.

Pilar Carballeira died when Aurora Rodríguez was fifteen. Though unexpected, her death did not unsettle her daughter. She had the feeling that she could breathe more freely, that for the first time she heard the servants laughing and singing in the house. Even Anselmo Rodríguez seemed more relaxed; he began to take Aurora seriously as a conversational partner. His circle of freethinkers met more and more often in his drawing room, rather than at the municipal club, and his daughter, who attended their meetings regularly, was the only female in attendance.

She read a great deal, more than the other members of the *tertulias,* with the exception of her father, had digested in their entire lives. She often felt that she understood the essence of things, and sensed that she was ahead of others, her peers at least, in book learning, in her restlessness, her wealth, her wish for a different life. Nevertheless, she saw no way out, already believed when she was half-grown that she had reached the end of her development. If only she were a boy; if only someone had encouraged her from childhood on, as she unconsciously had encouraged poor Pepito. But, for her, childhood was a lost time, and she belonged to the cursed sex that, as Hildegart was to write, slumbered along, scorned, without rights. *In this country public opinion has the effect of a strong current that pulls a woman along with it until she is caught in a whirlpool that finally sucks her into the depths. Indeed: look at the talents, the capabilities, the moral and spiritual greatness of Spanish women, which are crushed and allowed to wither by the public!* Public opinion also ruled the *tertulias* held at the Rodríguez house. No sooner had they discussed some bold new paradigm for society, which the lawyer was feeding them bit by bit, than the topic of the status of women came up, and suggestions to improve it ("with the permission of Señorita Aurora") were rejected: *Break the chaste woman's shin and lock her in.*

Aurora Rodríguez didn't feel herself locked in but locked out. What was open to her? What was there that she could do? *With few exceptions the Spanish woman cannot support herself. The earnings of a seamstress or a washerwoman barely cover her expenses. In the factories, the women of Spain earn too little in general. They are treated either as temporary help or their husbands are hired before they are. A woman who performs heavy physical labor in the fields or mines or on road construction, etc., is paid less than men whether she works as hard as the man or even harder. Teachers are no better off; their salaries don't even cover their meals. Other than a few positions in the larger cities, they suffer great disadvantage, unless they have access to other income. The woman artist in Spain is also without means. Discrimination and insufficient education block her entry to the*

professions of architecture and sculpture; she makes cop-
ies of tasteless paintings for the nouveau riche, decorates
fans, jewelry boxes, and porcelain, but even that, of little
value at any rate, is the exception, for the men dominate
here also. It is similar in the field of music: only in the
big cities are there a few women who can keep their heads
above water by giving piano lessons. Among scientists
there are only men. If a woman excels in an area, which
is rarely the case, it is of little help to her; she cannot
earn a living; the barriers of public opinion and the law
cannot be overcome.

Aurora Rodríguez, who feared she would not go far in
life, was stirred by the idea of a communal household.
The heart of the new society! She drafted a plan, drew
in stables, living rooms, studies, rejected them the next
day, and sat down again to work. Everything must have
a purpose, nothing could be left to chance. Putting the
dunghill too close to the housing area would be det-
rimental to health, for example, and a cesspit was
dangerous to children. The silo, as was the custom in
Galicia, would need to be supported on columns, to dis-
courage mice and rats; but wouldn't that also mean a
heat loss and an unnecessary amount of construction
material? And the first three hundred families; should
they all live together in a single, spacious structure, or
be spread out in a number of houses? Perhaps a village
was the answer, with each family living separately. But
wouldn't that make their common labor more difficult,
and also the building of a true community? For if people
were isolated, the old habits would continue to survive—power, distrust, willfulness. And who would reg-
ulate the work, decide what had to be done—a general

assembly? That would require a lot of time. Should there be committees of the individual spheres of labor—agriculture, livestock, crafts? But then each person would become specialized, quickly losing an overview of things, and would have trouble switching over to another area if the work was no longer appealing. Perhaps each family should send a delegate? Then it would again be the men who would sit down together. And the children? They knew too little to be held responsible. On the other hand, they were the only ones who were growing up free, without the ballast of the old society that still survived in their parents.

Aurora Rodríguez often went to her father for advice. When, finally, he got tired of answering her questions, he referred her to the book from which he had taken his knowledge. Aurora read it with effort, a dictionary at her side. But in it also there were open-ended questions. She wrote to the publisher. Several months later an answer arrived: they could not be of help; the author of the work, Charles Fourier, had died in 1837. That's no reason, Aurora thought, to give up the idea. The people could still be found. Her father possessed the capital. The right land needed to be located. She began carefully reading the ads in the newspaper. After six weeks she found an offer that suited her purposes. In Castile, near Alcalá de Henares, to the east of the capital, there was an estate for sale, one hundred fifty hectares, much too small for three hundred families, but within reason, if Anselmo Rodríguez put up everything he owned. In the beginning a smaller estate would be better, even, its chances for success greater because it was manageable; in the beginning, until everything was set up, there would undoubtedly be problems. On top of which, the land on all sides lay fallow, as she found out on asking, and therefore could be leased if the project went well, perhaps even purchased.

Aurora, who had corresponded in secret with the owner, revealed this bit of news to her father following the evening meal. Contrary to her expectations, he was not enthusiastic. He only laughed. When he noted her disappointment, he tried to explain to Aurora how senseless the whole plan was.

I'm an old man. I have not done one day's physical labor my whole life long. I would be of no value to such an enterprise. It calls for men who are fit, young, strong. And you are still a child. You shouldn't take my opinions so literally. That's just something we talk about.

A year later Anselmo Rodríguez was dead.

3

On the day that Aurora Rodríguez reached legal age, she advertised in the local paper that she wished to have a baby; that the man wishing to father the child she was to bear should answer the ad; and that she was determined not to marry him or to enter into any other relationship with him that resembled marriage. To this Aurora added that anyone who was willing to participate in this brief alliance, limited to the procreative act, must be of sound mind and body, that is to say, above the vulgar mediocrity that ruled in the land.

On the day after the notice appeared, Aurora's older brother, the only one of the family who still made El Ferrol his home, slapped his sister in the face. He arrived drunk from the Royal Sailing Club, where his friends had commented on this piece of news, not sparing him their derision. Aurora didn't defend herself against his blows, nor did she cry out or retreat from him even one step. Her reaction sobered her brother up. He turned slowly and left their parental home.

That was the last time the two met. The next-to-last meeting, if one didn't count accidental encounters on the street, took place on the day of Anselmo Rodríguez's burial when, at the insistence of the older brother and her sister, his testament was read. As her younger brother, despite his youth, was somewhere in America seeking his fortune, his share of the inheritance was put in the custody of a procurator. The inheritance came at a very opportune time for the older brother, who was not engaged in any regular work. Josefa, who moved in the better circles of Parisian society, also needed the money to continue her extravagant way of life, now that José Arriola had made several poor business deals.

As she was only seventeen, Aurora Rodríguez was assigned a guardian. In accordance with her father's last wishes, the chosen man for this role was Dr. Ochoa, a dear if somewhat simple man who had served as the family's doctor for years. Aurora had no desire to leave the family home. But she had no choice but to move into a room in the doctor's house; it was unthinkable that she not do as she was bid. Besides, Ochoa's wife, in a childless marriage, looked forward to having female companionship. Aurora Rodríguez insisted, however, on visiting her father's library every day. Dr. Ochoa's wife didn't like this, felt herself cheated out of her diversion, and feared for the family's reputation. When she asked her husband to put his foot down, he limited his charge's study time in the family home to three hours daily, and warned Aurora not to neglect her societal duties, now that she was approaching a marriageable age.

Dr. and Señora Ochoa viewed with irritation the efforts she was now making to educate the lower classes.

Her attempt to instruct El Ferrol's socialistically in-
clined workers in reading and writing at the school for
adult education certainly met a quick end. Many men
showed up on the first evening, most of whom got up
and left the room when the girl introduced herself as
their teacher. The next time, she waited for her students
in vain. Aurora believed that this aversion had nothing
to do with her person and everything to do with her age
and sex. For this reason, she proposed to hold a series
of lectures that would foster among the workers a greater
respect for women. She considered contempt for women
to be one of her country's greatest evils. *Of all civilized
peoples, the Spanish are the least tolerant toward the female sex; they have therefore remained behind all other
European nations, and have excelled neither in the sciences nor in the arts.* The party functionaries turned
down her proposal. We would only do ourselves dam-
age. The workers want class struggle, not a war in their
own families. And that Frog, Fourier, whom she referred
to, was totally confused, a little bank clerk with fuzzy
ideas, whom Marx had tried to teach some manners.

Aurora Rodríguez didn't give up. She paid to have an
article printed in the newspaper, anonymously, in which
she denounced the single household and the indissolu-
bility of marriage as a disadvantage, also for men, *de-
vised as if by a third sex (the ruling one), to condemn the
other two to much unpleasantness.*

A young woman of high society, wrote the union's
education advisor in answer, who chose not to give her
name, can think up nothing better in the face of the
workers' plight than to demand the liberation of women!
As if there weren't more important things to be done!

This blasé miss from a respectable bourgeois home should try exchanging her modern, well-heated residence for the pitiful space in a shack. Or asking a washerwoman with five children what her greatest wishes are. Fairer wages, humane housing would be the answer! It is only bored women from rich families who go for men's throats. That's their choice. But they should spare us their intellectual outbursts.

Aurora was disappointed: she could expect nothing from the workers. Their leaders were concerned only with material needs. They could think no further than that.

Charity begins at home.

Nevertheless, the workers must shake off the burden of the old, of the retrograde. Observe a new morality, educate themselves.

One couldn't expect too much of them, after a ten- or twelve-hour workday, and then a damp hole to sleep in, and a horde of children at home.

Dr. Ochoa's nephew, Juan Pardo, a tolerant listener and exciting conversational partner, was attractive and, in contrast to other officers, modest and skeptical concerning the meaning and purpose of the Spanish army. His relatives welcomed the fact that he frequently appeared at their home. The quiet cavalry captain, respected by the recruits, and the educated young orphan from a good home made a handsome pair. They also seemed to like each other, even if their conversations, according to Señora Ochoa, extended beyond what was conventional. The topics that Aurora broached were somewhat eccentric, she was too serious and introspective in general, and sooner or later she would ruin her eyes reading. And she considered behavior that was becoming in a girl, such as concern for her complexion and an interest in elegant clothing, to be trivial.

Dr. Ochoa tried to dispel his wife's misgivings. Aurora's behavior was not a matter for concern, and was not without its effect on men, who wanted more than beauty and finery. She took after her father, at any rate. Old Rodríguez had also been peculiar.

Exactly, his wife replied. And later you'll say that I exerted too little influence over her.

Aurora showed a great interest in her guardian's work. She pestered him until he allowed her to accompany him on his rounds. Dr. Ochoa had a reputation for possessing a soft heart. He granted requests from workers or peasants without means to make house calls on family members who were ill, and in contrast to his colleagues, who at the very least took mutton, eggs, or sacks of potatoes in exchange for their services, he often refused payment. Most of the time, however, as he admitted to his charge, his skills were of little service. Either he was summoned too late, when the patient was already dying, or the impossible was expected of him: the mason with the broken arm had to return to the construction site the next day, the dock worker with pneumonia had to be well in twenty-four hours. Tuberculosis and consumption, particularly among children, were considered by Dr. Ochoa to be a national disgrace. He prescribed sojourns in the dry, clean air of the Castillian Sierras and hearty food, beef bouillon, for example. But the poor, Aurora noted, could not afford the means to health. Galicia's villagers have little to eat. They rarely have meat and even in the vineyard areas wine is a luxury. Nutrition consists mainly of bread, with vegetables cooked in a little oil. The men dream of a new Sunday suit in which, well-dressed, in their opinion, they can appear at church or the marketplace.

Decades later, Aurora Rodríguez told the journalist Eduardo de Guzmán, who was visiting her in prison, that it was during this period that she began to consider the full ramifications of procreation.

If only people didn't bring so many children into the world, she said to Juan Pardo. When one or two would do. Not many beyond that survive anyway.

What can you do? the man said. Children are a gift of heaven.

That's ridiculous, cried Aurora Rodríguez. It's just the result of a biological act!

Oh, Aurora, let us have our little bit of romanticism.

With this kind of romanticism you won't change the world.

How, then?

Only with reason and discipline.

That's been tried already by many. And they failed.

Because they weren't up to the task.

That's unavoidable.

But it's possible. You have to proceed totally logically. Choose the parents carefully. Then the reproductive act. And, from that point on, total control. From the moment of birth, all energy is concentrated on the child. The best education. No diversions. No indolence.

The man laughed. Aurora was silent. He looked at her.

Don't be angry. You've fallen in love with something that has neither flesh nor blood.

And she had thought that he wasn't like the others.

I understand. I appreciate what you wish to accomplish. But I don't want a savior. *One* Jesus Christ was enough.

It would have to be a girl, anyway, Aurora said. Because it's also about women. Above all.

Following her twenty-third birthday, Aurora Rodríguez began to sell her share of the family inheritance. Her scandalous newspaper offer made the rounds in the city. Aurora, who on reaching legal age had moved back into the family home and broken off with Dr. Ochoa's nephew, felt the consequences. Acquaintances ignored her greeting in public, looked right past her or crossed the street. Half-grown children ran after her making obscene gestures, and old women crossed themselves.

Men prowled outside the house at night. Once she was woken by an entire troop of soldiers; the bravest among them assured her, amidst the laughter of the others, that each one of them was man enough to give her a child.

And they weren't the worst. Aurora Rodríguez found even more disgusting those men who pretended to understand her, who claimed they only wanted to be of service, *as they were already undressing me,* as she told Guzmán, *with their eyes.* She thought of fleeing anywhere away from there, Madrid or Barcelona, disappearing in the big city, unknown, to catch her breath, get a lawyer to dispose of her inherited goods, until one day a priest appeared at the door.

He wasn't recognizable as one. In his mid-thirties,

tall, broad-shouldered, tanned, he looked more like a
sailor. Which he was, he said, namely a priest in the
merchant marine, and if he had accustomed himself
to not wearing his habit, that was because it was not
zealots who were needed on the Christian voyage, but
strong-armed men. On top of which, he was critical of
the Church, held a low opinion of the comfort offered by
eternity, and therefore valued more highly the attempt
to make this ocean of tears more bearable. Which was
the reason for his visit.

You've read the notice?

He had been at sea when it appeared. No, he had
heard two men in a tavern talking about it only yesterday. Made curious by their comments, he joined the
conversation and learned of the contents of the notice.

So you know what it's about?

The gist of it. He also knew that the man was to disappear from Aurora's life afterward. And that he would
not be allowed to see the child.

Doesn't that appear harsh to you?

In no way. On the contrary. As a priest, albeit one
who concerns himself with people's physical needs, and
as a sailor, it would be quite impossible for him to enter
into a long relationship, even if he wished to.

Without being asked by Aurora Rodríguez, the priest
explained that the moment had not yet arrived to estab-
lish the place and time of the corporeal union. He had
at least four months' vacation, during which they could
get to know each other better. The young woman would
then be able to judge his character, and would, of
course, have the right to reject him as her choice to
father her child. His health? Except for the usual child-

hood diseases, and typhus, which laid him low in Barbados for months, no other physical ailments occurred to him. There was no record of chronic illness or mental deficiency in his family. Unlike the majority of sailors, he had never had a venereal disease, even though he personally rejected the oath of abstinence for himself. Moreover, his physical condition could be observed from his appearance. But if this, his conduct, his manner, or the content of what he had said was unacceptable to Aurora Rodríguez, she should say so immediately. He would go, avoid contact with her in the future, and say nothing of their conversation to anyone.

No, no. Stay.

4

On a cool day in spring, Aurora Rodríguez stepped off the train in the North Station. Immediately upon arrival she took a horse-drawn carriage to a centrally located hotel, from which she took leisurely walks over the next few days, exploring the city. In 1914, Madrid had six hundred thousand inhabitants concentrated in a small area within the so-called Bulevares, the Viejas Rondas, and the foul-smelling river bed of the Manzanares. The city remained for many of its citizens what it had been up to the beginning of the century, a dusty, loud stretch of village in Mancha, but for Aurora Rodríguez it was a metropolis. The young woman saw streetcars for the first time, which had until recently been drawn by mules, six- and even seven-story buildings, coffeehouses that were overcrowded at all hours of the day, and libraries whose collections exceeded her expectations. It was the behavior of the passers-by, however, that impressed Aurora Rodríguez the most; every one of them, it seemed, pursued his or her destination in great haste and uncon-

cerned with the possibility of collision, which forced
Aurora, worried about the welfare of her unborn child,
to steer a clear path.

The city, unlike El Ferrol, had little industry. Nevertheless, the poverty behind the façades of the elegant
Barrio de Salamanca and the Gran Vía was easy to spot.
A stone's throw from the Royal Palace, on the banks of
the Manzanares, along the bridges over which led the
roads to Segovia and Toledo, lived the washerwomen,
the ragpickers, and the gypsies in shacks of board and
bits of brick. There was no electricity, potable water, or
sanitation. The living conditions in the so-called lower
city, in Hospital, Inclusa, and Latina, where the majority of the population lived in badly constructed, drafty
houses with open staircases, were almost as bad. On
each floor there were twenty to thirty families, three
generations most of them, and each family shared one
room, where they cooked, ate, slept, and often also
worked.

Aurora Rodríguez did not wish to settle in the center
of the city. The crowded conditions, the dirt, the semi-
darkness that prevailed even in the houses of the better
quarters would inhibit her daughter's—she would have
a daughter, she was certain of that—development. She
found what she was looking for outside the city, in
the northeast: a boardinghouse in La Guindalera, with
light, friendly rooms and a garden stretching behind the
house. The owners, a childless couple from Asturias,
were not disturbed by the single woman's pregnancy. At
least there would be life around the house, the man
said. Would the expectant mother be able to cover the
costs?

Aurora Rodríguez rented an entire floor.

At the advice of a lawyer esteemed for his knowledge of industry, she put half of her inheritance into stocks of mining companies and cellulose factories, whose prices were to go off the charts during the world war and the years following.

Otherwise, the young woman led a quiet life, trying to follow the maxims of the medical handbooks in all regards. She got up early, had larger breakfasts, avoiding coffee and other liquid stimulants, than was the custom in her land, and then took a walk through the fallow countryside between La Guindalera and the city. She moved very slowly, in order not to exhaust herself, breathing deeply, and returned home before noon, before the sun was at its peak. Then she read, stretched out comfortably on a sofa for one or two hours until it was time to eat lunch, ignoring the common custom of an expectant mother following her appetite and eating for two. She avoided beer and wine, sausage, vinegared salad, and spices. She also refrained from cheese and eggs and ate meat only three times a week. She replaced her usual fare with green vegetables, fruit, and various grains, such as rice, buckwheat, millet, and oats.

After the meal Aurora Rodríguez chatted with the other guests at the boardinghouse (a retired colonel, a widowed baker), restricting her contact with them to the exchange of pleasantries and platitudes, because of their widely divergent views on national as well as European events. She feared that, in confronting them on their alarming opinions, she would work herself into a state of agitation that would be harmful to the health of the child in her womb. In a guide for expectant mothers, Hildegart would later warn against *becoming emotionally excited during pregnancy. The mother-to-be absolutely must impose rest upon herself, in order not to harm her child. If she is a worker, she should avoid physical strain from the beginning; the woman from the wealthy household should abstain from balls and other societal obligations, change her way of life, that is. Emotional distress, sudden shifts in temperament and participation in sports during the first months could result in serious malformations for the child. The influence of the environment on the mental state of pregnant women is immeasurable as well. War, revolution, revolt, hunger, poverty, and plague lead to a higher percentage of damaged children.* When the Great War broke out in Europe toward the end of her pregnancy, Aurora went so far as to discontinue her daily reading of two or three evening papers. She didn't wish to threaten her life's work with alarming news even before it had begun. Besides, following the mutual slaughter of the several nations, she had no great expectations for any major changes after the war.

She also spent the majority of the afternoons outdoors, under the shade trees of the boardinghouse, where she was safe from the harmful effects of the sun. Only when it was evening did she venture a second walk, this time toward the east, out to the open countryside, but never for long. Just as she sought out nature, to enjoy its beauty, she banned anything that was gloomy and tawdry from her environment. At her request her landlords removed the cheap, tasteless prints from her walls and, against their will, a massive crucifix that hung at the head of her bed. On the opposite wall, Aurora Rodríguez put a reproduction of the "Venus de Milo," so that it was the first thing she saw on waking. She then painted in a face that better suited the torso. She worried about her habit of sleeping only on her right side, so she forced herself to change her position hourly, in order not to restrict her child's development.

Though she tried to avoid mood swings, Aurora often found herself in a state of deep dejection, above all at night, when she questioned her intention to bring into the world a child who was to set people free, or some of them at least. In the beginning, she was disturbed by her morning sickness after breakfast. Because nausea, according to the books available to her, occurs primarily in women of well-to-do families, she interpreted it as a sign of her soft nature, which could only prove harmful, she believed, to her child. When her condition improved and, toward the middle of her pregnancy, disappeared altogether, she then discarded that idea. And then she regretted having chosen the priest to impregnate her. What if he suffered from a venereal disease, despite his assurances to the contrary? *If the man is syphilitic, a healthy woman can bear a syphilitic child without having shown any signs of this terrible sickness herself.* As her pregnancy progressed, she also had doubts about whether the child would indeed be a girl. She had heard that in the last weeks before menstruation the ovum's strength is at its weakest and, therefore, the majority of children conceived during this period are female. But she had disregarded this fact at the time of the final, decisive meeting. What would she do with a boy? *She wanted an offshoot of herself, a second Au-*

rora, a happier, more successful self. I was supposed to be freer, more munificent, more courageous, capable of organizing things according to my, her, wishes. I was to be strong, clever, creative, and also engaging, everything she herself failed in, for, owing to her upbringing, she had come in contact only superficially with what was meaningful. And though she well knew how the world should be constituted, she possessed neither the strength nor the prerequisites to form it in her own image. I was supposed to give her the feeling of having a true connection to the world.

In the last weeks of her pregnancy, Aurora Rodríguez maintained her new lifestyle. In her sixth month she had contacted a midwife who came highly recommended, in order to be able to call on the woman if the birth was premature.

On the evening of the eighth of December she felt a light pain in the small of her back that quickly moved to the front of her body, increasing in force. Aurora called for her landlady and asked her to contact the midwife. Until she arrived Aurora walked around the apartment, just as she had been advised. The midwife appeared just as her water broke, in a strong flood of yellowish amniotic fluid. Aurora Rodríguez, at the advice of the midwife, took a position on the side that was most comfortable for her, and tried with all her might to surrender to the contractions that were coming. After the third time she bore down the midwife assured her that she could already see the top of the baby's head, thick with hair. Soon thereafter the head appeared; the shoulders followed the next contraction. The midwife, who assisted the birth with few, but comforting, words, cut the umbilical cord, bathed the infant and wrapped it in warm diapers while Aurora rested until the discharge of her afterbirth.

An easy birth, the midwife said. And a healthy girl. What will you call her?

5

Eighteen months later, in May 1916, Aurora Rodríguez entered her daughter's name in the city's registry of births. She had hesitated, for a long time, before taking the step that many advised her to take; she feared that the girl would suffer disadvantage because she was illegitimate. To sidestep official channels, the presentation of certificates, and negative reactions, Aurora, giving in to sudden inspiration, gave the child's name as Carmen, but always called her daughter Hildegart, the garden of wisdom, because one's name, she later explained in court, was capable of influencing one's fate.

From the first day on, Aurora attempted to bestow upon the girl an exceptional upbringing. With everything in her power, she encouraged Hildegart's play drive, for as she knew, a child at play was putting its energy to practical use, studying its surroundings, making experiments, trying out its accrued observations and growing in mind and strength. In the beginning she regretted that her daughter had been born in winter, so that her first months of life were spent in a cold season. But she was soon convinced that low temperatures were no reason to keep Hildegart indoors. The neighbors could only shake their heads when they saw the child kicking and waving on a blanket in the garden.

Aurora Rodríguez, however, said that the body temperature, like that of animals, would adapt to cold, would sink, that is. But freezing was out of the question. On the contrary: in order to avoid the cold, the child must keep moving energetically. And that, in turn, would foster its dexterity, and with that, its reason.

And, sure enough, Hildegart never caught cold. When spring came, mother and daughter spent long hours outdoors. Aurora, who wished to have nothing to do with a baby carriage because it would limit movement and perception of the environment, commissioned a cabinetmaker to construct a playroom, a movable quadrangle with padded interior, a portable school with several bells at eye level. The child crawled around in it naked, which was judged indecent in those surroundings, and soon, without any help from her mother, pulled herself upright and in this way learned to walk before the end of her first summer.

At night, mother and daughter slept in the open, protected from inquisitive looks by canvas stretched between poles. Aurora Rodríguez tried to make clear to her landlady, who was annoyed by this peculiarity, that air baths, because they raised the body's oxygen intake and carbon-dioxide output, were extremely good for the health. In Central Europe and south of the Alps they were very common. Try it. The woman turned away in shock and crossed herself.

As often as Hildegart would allow her time for it, Aurora Rodríguez again turned her attention to public events. She followed the course of the war, which affected her country only indirectly, but she was more interested in its influence on events taking place in the protectorate of Morocco, where Spain's military presence appeared senseless and criminal to her, but it also worked as an opportunity to hasten the demise of the corrupt monarchy. Aurora hired a girl to take care of Hildegart, so that she could leave the house by herself, primarily to attend lectures at the Ateneo given by Spain's most eminent intellectuals. But she went grudgingly, for she didn't trust the maidservant to adhere to her own principles of upbringing in her absence.

Aurora Rodríguez considered all conventional dealings with children to be wrong. The tendency to employ grammatically false, diminutive-laden, artificial speech was as much a horror to her as the false modesty in awkwardly describing natural functions, such as bodily excretions and the organs concerned with them, as pee-pee and caca and popo. And the toys! Women from the neighborhood arrived with porcelain dolls, doll dish sets, and pink silk ribbons, and it was hard for the maid to obey Aurora and lock away the gifts.

The young mother took notice of every little thing, too much notice in many people's opinion. She didn't like for anyone to pick up Hildegart and saw to it that, when she fell down, she stood up unassisted. One day, to the surprise of the other residents, she had two cart-loads of sand and one cartload of gravel delivered to the garden, declaring that this was the most sensible recreation for Hildegart. There were also building blocks and bright-colored pieces of wood in the form of letters in the alphabet, which spelled out words if correctly assembled. The first word that Hildegart put together without help, her mother later told the journalist Guzmán, was v-i-d-a, life.

If Aurora Rodríguez obeyed the advice of the city's few enlightened pediatricians and the serious works of naturopathy, she nonetheless rejected them in one point: she seldom allowed Hildegart to play with other children. If it was unavoidable, because her refusal would be taken as brusque rejection, she soon found a pretext to withdraw her daughter from the company of others. Aurora explained to a well-known doctor who had observed her behavior and drawn her attention to the importance of communal play, that the wrong upbringing was contagious.

There were moments when Aurora Rodríguez was ambivalent about her mission. At Hildegart's birth, for example, she had felt, at having the tiny naked creature next to her, only happiness, and the explicit wish to protect this being, who had only her and existed only through her, to help her but never to force her to do anything, ever. And later, also, she was overcome at times by her desire to cuddle Hildegart for no reason at all, to devote herself to her daughter without regard to her plans for her upbringing, which allowed no time for idleness or aimless activity. She often felt the desire to transcend time itself, only to live for this moment when her daughter slept next to her, with her tiny hand in hers, or began to imitate her, her voice, the way she wrinkled her forehead, the way she opened a book.

Though she was later to deny it, it cost her no small effort to control these moments of *weakness*. Aurora

Rodríguez spoke to her daughter from the day of her birth on, unconcerned whether her daughter could understand her or not. She also immediately acquired for her a blackboard and chalk, and cut out the letters of the alphabet and glued them on cardboard. She pointed out numbers and letters to the child, just as she pointed out objects. That is a house. That is a tree. That is an A. And that, 5. When, at two, Hildegart began to be bored by the stringing together of letters, Aurora gave her a portable typewriter. When her mother worked at her desk, writing articles that she never attempted to publish, Hildegart sat in a high chair next to her at the same table, used the same paper, equally silent and focused.

The Madrid branch of the Underwood typewriter firm, authorized to award officially recognized certificates of typing proficiency, one day received a letter from Aurora Rodríguez announcing that her daughter possessed the skills necessary for such a certificate.

An employee of the company, who found his way to the boardinghouse a week later, thought it was a joke when Aurora Rodríguez asked him to administer the test to her three-year-old daughter. At first he laughed, then he accused the woman of wasting his time, said she was crazy, and threatened to charge her for his visit. It was Aurora's determination alone that forced him to stay. He gave the child a sample letter to copy; Hildegart passed the test within the specified time. After recovering from his shock, the man suggested that Aurora allow the company to capitalize on her daughter's abilities, for a sum, of course. Aurora Rodríguez declined. In the days following, representatives of the firm, and finally the director himself, also tried to convince her. When the pleas and offers proved fruitless, an editor appeared who, notified by the company of the sensation, wanted to publish an article on the *Wunderkind*. Aurora closed the door in his face.

From time to time it occurred to Aurora that her own abilities were no longer sufficient to expedite Hildegart's development to the extent she desired. She had encouraged her daughter's potential, but she knew her limits. Tutors would have to cover those areas Aurora Rodríguez could never penetrate: mathematics, physics, foreign languages. She placed ads in socialist papers, with success. The men, initially astonished at the tender age of their pupil, were soon enthusiastic in their task.

One of the tutors, Don Matías, felt very close to the child. He had studied in Germany, and as a result intended to translate the works of the philosopher Karl Christian Friedrich Krause, greatly respected in Spain's intellectual circles, until he found Nietzsche's work to be far more important. He was the only one who dared to express to Aurora Rodríguez his doubts on this or that method of upbringing. He occasionally noticed signs of exhaustion in Hildegart. Wasn't she overburdening the child? Wasn't it better to proceed more slowly with the material, not only to avoid repletion, and with it a loss of interest, but also to allow Hildegart an opportunity to be with others her age and to develop socially?

Aurora rejected his concerns. One's receptivity, she maintained, is limited. The years of growth, the first seven years, must be taken advantage of. If the mental capabilities were not utilized or were underutilized, they would fade, never again to be recovered. She had observed that in herself; despite all her efforts to compensate, under the most favorable of conditions, for the obstacles set up for her in childhood, her intellectual ambitions had scarcely been met. But she was still capable of encouraging them, she informed him.

Don Matías, who secretly had great respect for her, did not agree with her view of herself. But Aurora Rodríguez persisted, citing the inferiority of women in general, which, by the way, she said, was also mentioned by your esteemed Herr Nietzsche, who, of course, did not comprehend the deeper causes of this inferiority. The child must be taken seriously. I require of Hildegart no more than I would require of myself under similar circumstances.

Nevertheless, you should be more tolerant. The maid tells me that you don't allow your daughter to play with the other children.

Julia, you'll forgive me, is stupid and uneducated. Those children's parents are just as stupid. Should I give in and sabotage Hildegart's development? Later, when her education has been established, she shall, she must, open herself to the world. Until then, your company, and mine, are enough. And we'll get a few pets, dogs or cats. You can also learn about community through them.

6

Sixteen years later, when, to the murmuring of those in attendance, her attorney declared that it had come to his attention that Hildegart's natural father was in the courtroom, Aurora Rodríguez would remember the morning she heard someone call her name in the swirl of pedestrians, under the high voices of the newsboys and the hoarse cawing of the blind men selling lottery tickets. She had stopped and turned around. The woman timidly smiling at her seemed familiar. But Aurora couldn't place her among her acquaintances. The woman called out again.

Aurora? Aren't you Aurora Rodríguez?

I'm sorry, Aurora said. I can't remember at the moment where I've had the pleasure.

Blanca Varela, the woman said, your neighbor in El Ferrol. I had great regard for your parents. What a coincidence.

The woman from Galicia followed her, not without hesitation, into the next coffeehouse, and Aurora Rod-

ríguez resigned herself to listening to news of her home-
town. Señora Varela told her that a new shipyard had
been approved; that the late, beloved canon had been
succeeded by a younger, gruffer one; that the municipal
clubhouse and the socialist adult-education center had
been closed, the one owing to dilapidation, the other to
agitation against the authority of the state; and that a
certain Señora Pelayo, you remember her, don't you?
had died a sudden death. It was said that her husband
had played a role in it. But the doctors weren't saying
anything.

How were Dr. Ochoa and his wife? As far as I know,
they are both well. He still has his practice, but can no
longer be relied on. His age. None of us are getting any
younger. Except for you, of course, Aurora. You look
splendid.

Aurora Rodríguez, who wished to put this sudden en-
counter behind her as soon as possible, inquired about
her brother. The other woman hesitated.

So he has remained a good-for-nothing, Aurora said.

You know how it is. But he has a good heart. He's
foolish, and doesn't keep the best company. A man he's
often seen with recently caused a scandal. The biggest
scandal we've had in a long time.

What was it? Aurora asked. Fraud, theft?

Worse.

Murder?

The other woman looked around her. Then she low-
ered her voice.

A sailor, she said, posing as a priest. He's supposed
to be very cultivated. He insinuated himself into the
best circles. Now no one wants to have anything to do

with him. He has a brother in El Ferrol who supported him. He has repaid him poorly. The daughter of the family, not even twelve years old—he molested her. When her father found out about it he almost lost his mind. Ran through town with a pistol in his hand. He came within a hair's breadth of killing your brother because he couldn't tell him where the monster was. But the man had already disappeared. Allegedly, he is now in Madrid.

Here?

Mrs. Varela nodded. The police are looking for him. It's in all the papers.

What does he look like?

His appearance reveals nothing of his character. He is tall and strong, good-looking. Eloquent and knowledgeable on many topics. In spite of that, it must have occurred to the men he was acquainted with that something about him wasn't quite right. The way he railed at the church, for example, though he presented himself as a priest.

He wasn't one?

Once. But they only found that out later. Also that he had embezzled money.

Aurora Rodríguez tried to hide the shock that she felt. She motioned to the waiter as the woman was trying to find out more about Aurora's life with some question about her health.

I'm fine, Aurora Rodríguez said, I'm studying and am in the process of moving from my apartment. That, unfortunately, is why I cannot extend an invitation to visit me during the next few days.

The woman thanked her. I am returning tomorrow anyway. Shall I say hello to anyone for you?

In a sudden burst of openness Aurora declared that she was very much alone, wished to see no one, and that she had left nothing behind in El Ferrol worth remembering. She then stood up and left the coffeehouse without a word of farewell.

Look, the maid said, how funny the bees are flying around.

They're working, Hildegart answered. They're bringing the male pollen to the stigma. Then a tube grows down to the egg and then it's fertilized.

You certainly know a lot.

I know a lot more.

Julia Sanz was only half listening. She was watching the photographer in front of them, who was leisurely unpacking his tripod and setting up his box camera. A dignified man. What an interesting profession! And he often looked over at them.

Why is that man staring at you? Hildegart asked.

Maybe he likes me.

Maybe he wants to fertilize you, the little girl said.

Not so loud.

Why are you turning red?

I'm not turning red.

Yes you are.

Julia tried to change the subject. I've never been photographed.

But fertilizing people is different from fertilizing plants.

Hildegart! Be quiet. The man. He can hear us.

He has a penis, Hildegart said, and he sticks it in your vagina. And then semen comes out and fertilizes an egg and then a child begins to grow in your stomach. And then it comes out and plays with me. Can it play with me? Please, promise me!

Now that's enough, the maid said. She stood up and took Hildegart by the hand. Come, we're going home.

At home, where Aurora Rodríguez was pacing back and forth in a fit of emotion, it occurred to her for the first time to put an end to her daughter's life and her own also. She cursed the moment when the false priest had entered her life, and was weighing several different manners of death when Hildegart rushed into the room and threw her arms around her. Aurora was so touched that she bridled her bitter feelings. Until now, she thought, the child has exhibited only positive characteristics; why should the destructive influence of her procreator win the upper hand? Her eyes filled with tears as Hildegart was telling her that Julia Sanz knew nothing about conception. Don't cry, said Hildegart. I've already told her all about it. Aurora pressed the child to her.

Today is a special day, she said. You can make a wish.

I wish, I wish—I had a child!

As many children as you want.

Aurora turned to the maid. In October Hildegart is going to school.

The next day Aurora Rodríguez regretted her promise. But she could not set a bad example for Hildegart, could not take it back. Against her will she began to look for an acceptable school. It took a long time for her to find anything that even halfway met her expectations. The few state institutions, more custodial than educational, were overfilled and their sanitary conditions were highly questionable. Their directors also absolutely refused to accept children under six years of age. Religious institutions, on the other hand, were willing to educate a four-year-old, but were put off by the fact that, as an illegitimate child, Aurora's daughter remained in a state of sin. On top of which, they considered humility before God to be the first principle of education, and Aurora could imagine that Hildegart's interest in the biological facts of life would not prove compatible with the distorted way religious obscurants would represent sexuality. As she did not approve of the Church and considered the practices of religious ceremony to be deleterious, Aurora eliminated this possibility. In the end, she decided to found a school together with other parents, but did not dare to make this intention public, because she feared that she would put Hildegart's father, should he really be in Madrid hiding from the authorities, onto her and her daughter's trail. Only later did it occur to her that the man would have had no trouble locating her, if he had really wished to.

Hildegart's tutors, and other highly-placed liberals whom Aurora consulted, helped her to find parents interested in the project. Many of them appeared on the evening of their first meeting, and were totally supportive of what she had to say about her intentions and the focus of the future academy. But the more concrete the undertaking became, after Aurora Rodríguez found an appropriate building to lease and began searching for suitable teachers to hire, the more interest waned. They hesitated to give their final approval, raised objections that didn't stand up under scrutiny, and finally were of the opinion that the status quo would suffice.

Aurora had no choice but to look around for another school. She finally found one near the university, in the city's northwest section. The director, a member of the Piarist teaching congregation, explained to her that the school's goal was to prepare the children for responsible positions.

Our faculty pays special attention to subjects that are too often neglected—the sciences, that is. And foreign languages, in particular French and Latin, uncommonly useful to math instruction owing to their high degree of absolute rules. We are interested in independent learning and not simply a regurgitation of the material. Our single concession to traditional education is that the students are segregated by sex.

And religion? Aurora asked.

It's not so bad, the man said, laughing. We must, of course, proselytize young heathens.

And so Hildegart was baptized.

She entered school before the end of her fifth year. To save her the long trip, Aurora Rodríguez moved to an apartment in the Calle Galileo, ten minutes from the school. In the beginning, Hildegart missed the large garden of their boardinghouse; the nearby East Park was a poor substitute. But her mother decided that exercise was no longer so important. The time could be used for learning instead.

The leavetaking from La Guindalera was difficult for no one except Hildegart. The owners had grown fond of the child, it was true, but they were nevertheless glad to be rid of the mother, who was often critical, consid-

ered many things in need of improvement, and in the
end held fiery debates with the retired colonel, despite
their asking her to ignore him and his cantankerous
opinions. Aurora Rodríguez had tried. She had succeeded for a while, enduring even his childish delight
in the bloody suppression of the mass strikes of 1917.
But then she told herself that she was setting a bad example for her daughter in letting him trumpet his
twisted views unchallenged. It also gave her satisfaction
to see that her predictions proved correct, that the Central Powers, long victorious, were moving toward final
defeat.

Nor was Julia Sanz unhappy with the move, for it offered her more social opportunities. Because of the out-
of-the-way location of the boardinghouse, she had
usually spent her days off together with mother and
daughter, and she longed to pass her free time on Sundays in the carefree company of her own kind. She now
also hoped to escape the books, the readings that Aurora Rodríguez recommended to her, which she fell
asleep over in the evenings after the first page.

After one week, Hildegart was promoted to the second class, and six months later she again skipped a
year. Aurora's fear that her daughter would be bored at
school, would become lethargic from the lack of chal-
lenge, proved unfounded. The company of the other,
older children compensated Hildegart for the pressure
she was subjected to at home by her mother and tutors.
But this company also held danger; therefore, before
Hildegart could ask, Aurora voluntarily told her that her
father had been an intelligent and noble man, who had
had the misfortune to lose his life in an accident at sea.

But Aurora couldn't get around making allowances

for customs that she herself rejected. When her fellow students had their first communion, Hildegart didn't want to be left out. She begged for a candle, a white dress, a myrtle wreath. Aurora Rodríguez considered it all to be nonsense.

There is no God.

No, Hildegart said. But if I go without them, the others will laugh at me.

Her mother gave in. Better this, she thought, than give her the feeling her whole life long that she missed something.

After communion Hildegart, not seeing what the swallowing of unleavened bread had to do with serious phrases and measured steps, ran out of church without waiting for the end of the mass.

Although the law did not provide a deferment of religious instruction, the director asked Aurora, at the urgent request of the teacher, not to allow her daughter to attend these classes. The other children's moral sensibilities were endangered, he said, because Hildegart was causing a disturbance with her questions about God's sex and her doubt about the immaculate conception. The religion teacher dreaded each class, broke out in a sweat. He didn't know what to do.

Aurora informed her daughter. All right, Hildegart said, I won't go anymore. I'm not angry at him. But he tells us fairy tales.

7

Aurora Rodríguez also maintained that Hildegart did not lack the company of others, of paternal friends who were well-disposed to her and recognized her extraordinary gifts. There was old Méndez Bejarano, for instance, Professor of the History of Law at Madrid's Central University, who reminded Aurora strongly of her father. His lectures were particularly exciting to her and to Hildegart, who got a dispensation from the Minister of Education at thirteen to begin the study of law, which Aurora considered absolutely necessary for a political career.

The gentle, white-haired man was considered by his colleagues to be an eccentric, who attracted students only because he graded leniently and was incorruptible in his judgments. He had earned their respect with his courage in openly criticizing powerful institutions, like the army, the Church, even the monarchy itself, Alfonso XIII and his viceroy, General Primo de Rivera, who had ruled since the coup.

Méndez seldom varied his lectures. He began each
hour with a tribute to the *comuneros*, who had been defeated three hundred and fifty years before because the
civil nobility had betrayed the middle class. Then, in
1873, when the republic was founded, the middle class
had betrayed the masses. The bourgeoisie had at first
supported the federalism demanded by the proletariat.
But, when they scented the danger of social change,
they secretly opted for a centralization of power, empha-
sizing the necessity for an authoritarian structure by citing the Carlinian volunteer corps in the north, who were
taking a stand on religion and the monarchy. Pí y Margall, the great statesman who believed in free and independent means of production, and in autonomous
cantons that would be equally entitled to exchange
wares, had attempted to mediate, as he knew that only
a union of middle-class and proletariat could prevent
the rise of the military and block the threat posed by the
Carlists. He resigned when he recognized that the bourgeoisie was not interested in reform, that its ally was
considered a greater threat than the return to monarchy
and centralism. His successor to the office of president,
Nicolás Salmerón, buried the Republic, bombarded the
cities of Andalusia, as well as Alicante, Valencia, and
finally, in the bloodiest battle of all, Cartagena, where
the Canton of Murcia had proclaimed itself an autonomous republic. In January, 1874, Cartegena was taken
by a rabble of soldiers, France turned over to the government the Communards who had fled to North Africa,
and they remained in Africa as forced labor. Salmerón,
the gravedigger, the bureaucratic murderer, the white-
collar butcher, went so far as to present himself as a

republican, a republican in spirit, mind you, a monarchist in deed. So the Middle Ages once again took control of this land, and has not let go even today, with Primo's despicable dictatorship serving the monarch as a final measure against the will of the people.

The students, caught up in this discourse, began to stamp their feet in approval. A warden, alarmed by this sudden disturbance, stuck his head in the door and laid a finger on his lips in warning.

Méndez, who had talked himself into a rage, ended his lecture and called upon the students for opinions, questions, additional comments.

After a moment's hesitation, someone raised his hand.

Primo de Rivera is doing the best he can. He is getting power stations built, and streets; he has ended the war in Morocco and restored order. Had he not appeared, there would no longer be a Spain. With the ceaseless assassinations, a civil governor here, a bishop there, a strong arm was needed to stay the collapse of the state.

There is no more stupid opinion than that, Mendez answered. The nations want freedom, then they'll live peacefully with one another. The only thing the dictatorship guarantees is selling out the country. British companies welcome the ban on unionization, the Church embraces the General for leaving them their cloisters, their prebends, their schools, for banning troublemakers to the Canary Islands, for sending others into exile, where they die of broken hearts.

But Don Mario, the student continued, despite his fellow students' attempts to quiet him, you yourself are here. There is censorship, that is true. But you are treated well. True, there aren't free elections. But this class is proof that one can still speak freely at the universities. You don't mince words. Nor does your colleague Besteiro, nor De los Ríos.

First, I'm an old man, Méndez replied. The dictatorship doesn't profit from throwing a seventy-year-old into prison or out of the country. Second, Primo de Rivera knows very well how far he can go. If you strip the threads of a screw, it won't hold. And, as far as my Socialist colleagues are concerned, I only wish to remind you that their union, unlike the much more powerful union of anarcho-syndicalists, is not banned, and that the Socialist Largo Caballero, called the Lenin of Spain by those who don't know any better, is the sole civilian in Primo's directorate. That is an insult to every worker.

The Socialists, said Hildegart, are in the process of correcting their mistakes. They have learned.

Learned? Méndez asked. That would be nice. But I don't believe it. Their leaders are now distancing themselves from the dictator because they will lose the workers otherwise. Actions, says Pí y Margall, are nothing more than a transformation of ideas, and it is ideas that the Socialist politicians lack.

Hildegart disagreed. I would concur with Marx, who said the opposite, more precisely than Pí y Margall— that societal existence determines consciousness. Poverty, which has increased precipitately in the last years, has demonstrated to many the urgent need for a republican form of government. But a republic, even a federal republic, cannot be the final goal. If it is, then the mil-

itary and the religious fanatics will rise up again. Co-
operatives of independent communes can be created
only if the old practices disappear: the domination of
women by men, the myriad influences of religious education, the taboo on sexuality. Otherwise the old will
survive in the guise of the new. I know what socialism
wants. But federalism is vague, hazy.

I am easily inspired, said Professor Méndez at the
end of the class. Perhaps our generation was too impul-
sive. Señorita Hildegart is much more analytical, despite her youth. Maybe the future belongs to her.

On the evening of December 7, 1928, after she had
helped the maid set the table, Hildegart went to her
mother to tell her that a period in the timetable she had
set for herself had ended. The next day was her four-
teenth birthday, and she felt strong enough now to take
part in political events. Aurora Rodríguez asked her
what form this participation would take.

I want to make known my opinions on the events of
the day, publicly, Hildegart said. In the press, at meetings. I will hold lectures. Take part in demonstrations.
Mobilize the students.

Alone? Aurora asked. Without belonging to a party?

That's useless, said Hildegart. Whoever is alone
loses. I've thought about it for a long time. I belong in
the youth group, in the union.

With the Socialists? asked Aurora.

I know what you think of them, Hildegart said. You
think the same as Professor Méndez.

There are other parties that fight for the republic.

For the republic. But for nothing else.

And the Federalists. Aren't they more radical?

Romantics, the girl said, who can't distance themselves from the past. They live in the last century.

On the first of January Hildegart, having disregarded her mother's misgivings, applied for acceptance to the Socialist Youth. Then she went with Aurora to the Calle del Piamonte, to the union's headquarters. The man Aurora Rodríguez asked for assistance was busy stamping the union books of a long line of workers who were paying their dues. My daughter wishes to join.

The man studied Hildegart. Is she even housebroken yet?

Aurora was incensed: Are all Socialists as uncouth as you?

The man laughed. We're no kindergarten.

My daughter is a student.

That's something else altogether. Just a moment. I'll be with you in a minute.

While he continued his work, Aurora and Hildegart looked around. A meeting was taking place in a room on the second floor. Men in blue work smocks—three or four hundred, Aurora guessed—were loudly interrupting each other. When from the podium a bell rang, it took a long time before it was quiet.

Comrades! We have come to vote. Whoever is for the strike should stand up. A scraping of chairs, only a few remained seated, looking around, wildly gesticulating.

The majority for, said the speaker.

One of those who had remained seated asked to speak. I consider the vote a huge mistake. Strikes and more strikes. As if they were the answer to everything. Enough of this being led around by the nose! Direct action, he yelled, then they'll stop laughing at us.

We aren't anarchists, called someone from the back

of the room. Such methods are self-defeating! Keep quiet, the decision was clear-cut.

The ladies should forgive him. He, the cashier, had not wished to insult them earlier. But it was so seldom that women, well-to-do women, one saw that at first glance, wandered in here. At best, a few women workers from the textile mills. And they came only because of the medical insurance, because we have contracts with many doctors and pharmacists. But it is risky to become a member; if the owners find out you can kiss your job goodbye. And you won't find another so quickly. Only the masons and the printers have caught on, the man said. There's not one of them who isn't with us. And the *patrón* respects that. For that reason, they only work eight hours a day and start with a salary of ten silver *reales*.

On their way to the theater and the workers' library, which the man wanted them to see, Hildegart asked if there were also students active in the union.

Very few. But I hope it will be different soon.

You can count on that, the girl said.

Aurora Rodríguez remained distrustful of what she called the bumbling of Socialist politics. But she tried to keep her reservations to herself. Nevertheless, she did instruct her daughter not to neglect her studies for her political engagement, and to push ahead with her work on the situation of women.

Already in 1927, at twelve years of age, Hildegart had won first prize in a contest sponsored by the city of Saragossa for her extensive comparative study of the relationships between Romeo and Juliet, Abelard and

Héloïse and the lovers of Teruel. It was three years before the work appeared in book form, because the jurors couldn't agree whether or not its publication went against the laws of the dictatorship, owing to the author's age as well as to the delicate topic. In it, Hildegart attempted to define her concept of love precisely. In the case of Romeo and Juliet, she wrote, heart had won out over head; their love was madness. With Abelard and Héloïse it was exactly the opposite, convention conquered passion, individual security was more important than the security of the other; it was not love, therefore, but selfishness. Only in the ancient legend of Teruel, of Diego and Isabel, did she discover moderation, the balance of emotion and reason. And, even if their fate ended in death, their love remained pure, serene, unclouded.

When Andrés Saborit, editor-in-chief of the Socialist party paper, received his first manuscript from Hildegart, he assumed, because of her uncommon name, that it was the pseudonym of a well-known author, used to avoid difficulties with the censors. Fascinated by its subject, an obituary honoring a French feminist, he wrote to Hildegart, proposing further contributions and hastening to add that he would like to make the acquaintance of the unknown author. Hildegart appeared in the company of her mother, who had difficulty correcting Saborit's mistaken impression that it was she who was the author of the article. Saborit could use a staff writer, or better, a woman who could examine the topics, long neglected by the Socialists, of the emancipation of women, sexual hygiene, and the role of youth in the coming societal reform. The fact that Hildegart

violated taboos was easy to justify to the party leadership as long as the Socialists represented the opposi-
tion, if barely tolerated.

Like all other newspapers, *El Socialista* had to sub-
mit each issue to a censor, who appeared at the printer's
late every night to begin checking the articles that
had already been typeset. He was a corpulent, short-
winded, bald man with pasty skin and a volatile temperament. If he was pleased with the meal that the
apprentice brought him from the nearest restaurant, it
could happen that every article made it to print. But
that could backfire the next day, if his superior scolded
him for his negligence, in which case, despite dessert
and a glass of brandy, he found something subversive in
every harmless report, football games and theater pre-
mières included. Because the editors refused to substitute other, inoffensive articles for the censored ones at
the last minute, the paper often appeared with empty
spaces. Or an article broke off in the middle; sometimes
only one word was missing, which the readers could
easily guess from the context, and that particularly an-
gered the authorities.

Hildegart often didn't recognize her own articles. Occasionally, only the title and her name at the bottom of
it were evidence that the space had been hers. Aurora
Rodríguez surmised that Saborit was not at all concerned with the subject matter; rather, he was playing
with people's belief that any paper so severely censored
must be attacking the dictatorship in a particularly un-
compromising manner. Hildegart was one of the decoys
for reformist, compromising politicians. Her daughter
rejected her suspicions and reminded her of the free-

dom with which she spoke at meetings. The party youth
stood behind her, lent substantial support to her demand for the abolition of all laws antagonistic toward
women.

At the university, Hildegart soon gathered around her
a group of like-minded students. She was respected,
even though the students thought it odd that her mother
never left her side, even when she plastered up posters
at night and was chased by the police in the process.
The Congress of the Youth Organization convened in
September, 1929. Hildegart, at fourteen, was the
youngest delegate. When the Catalonian section nomi-
nated her for vice-president, the thunderous applause
that followed made a vote superfluous.

In January of the following year, the dictator, whom
even part of the army refused to support, was forced to
resign. King Alfonso named a general, Berenguer, to
head the Directorate. He hoped that a more accommo-
dating policy would split the enemies of the monarchy.
But it was already too late for that. Berenguer tried to
stem resistance to the dictatorship with a flood of legal proceedings. The bureaucracy collapsed under the
weight of everyone seeking to be brought to court for
incitement to riot, disturbance of the peace, or participation in an unauthorized demonstration. Two days after
her sixteenth birthday, when she attained the age at
which she could have legal action brought against her,
Hildegart was charged with lèse-majesté. In an article
in the Youth newspaper *Renovación*, she proposed that
the king's mistresses be sent to a home for wayward
girls.

The case never made it to court.

8

The twelfth of April, 1931, was a bright spring day. The morning sun shone down from a cloudless sky; it was nevertheless cool, a cold wind was blowing from the Guadarrama Mountains, and Aurora, who had just finished breakfast with her daughter, sat down at the window, pushing the curtains to one side.

Look, she said, the men are taking their canes for a walk.

And not a woman in sight, said Hildegart.

God forbid, the maid said. Who knows what will happen?

The men passing by on the street below wore their Sunday suits and the first straw hats of the season. The last elections had been held eight years before, confrontations were expected, and canes and hats could serve a certain purpose in the case of either attack or defense.

What could happen? Hildegart said. We will win. The monarchy is at an end.

They say the monasteries will be set on fire, Julia Sanz whispered. And the churches.

That's a lot of nonsense, said Aurora. You shouldn't believe everything you hear on the street.

In the afternoon she and Hildegart went to the central telephone exchange, where the journalists awaited the first election results from the provinces. They were bored, and also disappointed that everything had gone quietly at the polls. A few disturbances—how could you make a dramatic story out of that? Most of them had published zealous appeals in the last few days, urging their readers to vote for the candidates of the republican parties; but now they were skeptical, expressed their doubts that a dictatorship could be toppled by elections that they themselves had called for. Only the leftist radicals, young Guzmán, for example, were betting on victory, undauntedly prophesying the fall of the government; they were laughed at.

Partial results came in toward evening. In Barcelona the republican candidates had received seventy percent of the votes; the results in Valencia, Seville, and Bilbao were also overwhelming. In Saragossa and Valladolid, too. And finally in Madrid itself: ninety thousand votes for the Socialists and republicans, three times the votes cast for the monarchy. Hildegart laughed: even the court toadies had voted against the King.

The next day, Aurora Rodríguez and Hildegart went to the Calle del Piamonte. A detail of the civil guard was posted in front of Socialist headquarters, inside which people stood or sat crowded together in the corridors, at tables, on chairs and steps. But the guard did not refuse the women entrance; those in uniform appeared uncertain, seemed to be waiting for orders that didn't come. In the afternoon, a red flag was raised.

Then they heard that the King was packing his bags, that one of the princes had already fled to Gibraltar, that Berenguer had instructed the army to remain calm. The crowd streamed into the street. A worker, carrying a crudely sewn cloth with the colors of the republic, approached an officer and demanded that he salute the flag. The officer hesitated; finally he drew his sword and saluted. The people clapped and cheered the republic.

The two women rode the wave of enthusiasm and were carried along by the current of people who streamed toward the telephone exchange from the outskirts of the city. In front of the Ministry of the Interior the sentries fired into the crowd of demonstrators, who ignored the order not to come any closer. Hildegart didn't comprehend the danger, understood the shots to be a call to continue the assault; she was elated, her cheeks were flushed with excitement and energy. Aurora Rodríguez grabbed her arm and tried to pull her daughter away from the front lines, but she shared Hildegart's excitement. People, she called out to her, have finally begun to act. Groups advanced from the side streets, waving flags, yelling, gesticulating, women and children among them, and joined the others, streaming together, all of them. Without even a call to unite, they went, no, ran, neither charging nor hesitating, to the royal palace, over the Puerta del Sol, where the soldiers mingled with them, tearing the insignia of the monarchy from their caps and belts.

The crowd halted at the plaza. Others pushed their way in from the streets, not comprehending the sudden standstill, yelling to those in the front to find out why the demonstration had stopped. Young people wearing red armbands formed a chain in front of the palace, where the royal guard was entrenched. Hildegart recognized several of her comrades among them.

No provocation, the youth called, no unnecessary bloodshed now, when the republic is so close; composure, not senseless violence, to show the army, the whole land, the world even, that order is possible also without a king.

Aurora Rodríguez laughed bitterly. Your comrades, she said, do not understand the purifying power of force. They want culture, civilized behavior, to maintain a respectful distance of fifteen feet. I can see it already; nothing will change.

Hildegart contradicted her. The republic is of course not the end goal, but the precondition for change. You can't have everything right away. The masses want security, safety, even as they now put an end to the monarchy. Everything progresses slowly; habits are too deeply rooted in people for them to be able to trust a spontaneous outbreak of the people's will.

My comrades need me, she said, to safeguard the palace. She struggled to the front. Aurora Rodríguez didn't want to leave her alone, and followed.

The next day the King left the building through the back door. In Cartagena he boarded a cruiser that took him to France. Shortly thereafter, the Socialists joined the newly formed government. This decision was widely debated within the party. The Youth Organization expressed their suspicion that the bourgeois majority had offered them three ministries in order to be able to ignore the workers' demands without risk. Even the party leadership was divided. Should they force reform on the government by attack from the outside, or win influence through cooperation with it? Finally, those who supported a coalition government won out; their most powerful opponents, as Aurora Rodríguez ascertained, were appeased with high positions.

The master baker Manuel Cordero had supported the coalition. In the fall, Hildegart appeared together with him as a speaker at a Socialist rally in the workers' quarter of Carabanchel. Cordero reminded the crowd of the achievements of the republic, achievements that were, however, barely perceptible in the daily lives of workers, and promised immediate reforms: the forty-eight-hour work week, the introduction of a minimum wage, and a fight against price increases. Hildegart, whose abundant figure was one result of her sedentary existence as a student and writer, addressed the situation of women, education, and family planning. As she, Cordero, and Aurora traveled back to the city by trolley after the rally and were crossing the bridge over the Manzanares, the politician pointed to the shacks below and commented how horrible the accumulation of filth and misery was, a disgrace to the entire city. Aurora Rodríguez said nothing, as always when she and her daughter were in the company of a third person. But Hildegart, surprised and infuriated by the thoughtlessness with which a functionary of the party that had originated in sympathy with the disenfranchised had pronounced judgment, reprimanded Cordero sharply.

It is not these shacks that are a disgrace, but rather the conditions that brought them into existence. Not the sagging shanties, but the wealth that requires this poverty. Did Señor Cordero also declare his indignation at the palaces, villas, and elegant shops in such a loud voice?

At home, Aurora Rodríguez praised the decisiveness with which her daughter had reproached the man, but doubted that the politician, who was mute with embarrassment after Hildegart's retort, had spoken rashly, out of thoughtlessness or fatigue. Your comrades, she said, are now showing their true colors.

Hildegart disagreed. Local party chapters from all over the country are issuing invitations to have me come and speak on the emancipation of women and sexual hygiene—more than I can accept. These are sensitive topics that many people don't want to talk about. The Socialists here have held to their principles in spite of that.

Wait, Aurora said. You will see.

The two women had to flee the village of Matavenero, in which a cobbler by the name of García had founded a socialist educational society. A week before, the innkeeper's wife had given the priest a handwritten notice on which the cobbler issued an invitation to a lecture by *the illustrious Señorita Hildegart, vice-president of the Socialist Youth of Spain, author of the brochures* Limiting Population Growth, Sexual Education, *and* Sexuality and Love, *75 céntimos each.*

The priest forbade the innkeeper, under threat of excommunication into the third generation, to put his inn at the disposal of a campaign against God's well-established order. From the pulpit he also issued an urgent warning against temptation by the devil, who appeared in diverse forms and was capable of speaking in the beguiling voice of a young woman. The service was interrupted when the cobbler, who had gone to church because the innkeeper's sudden change of mind had made him suspicious, jumped out from behind a pillar and accused the servant of God of being a charlatan and a demagogue, at which the latter threw a crucifix at him.

When Hildegart and Aurora Rodríguez reached the village for the lecture, they were met by a shower of stones. Under cover of twilight, the cobbler took them, by a circuitous route, to his home at the other end of town, where five stalwart souls, all men, awaited them. Hildegart had barely begun her talk when loud voices were heard outside the house, someone rattled at the front door, and a stone as big as a fist crashed through the window and smashed against the wall near the girl. Mother and daughter quickly packed up the newspapers and books they had brought with them, the men rolled up their sleeves, and the cobbler's wife offered to accompany the two women to the next village. As a fight broke out in front of the house, Hildegart and Aurora ran across the fields with their skirts held high. Mud-spattered, they boarded an express train in León the next day for Madrid.

By coincidence, they were seated in the same compartment as the Socialist politician Julián Besteiro, with whom the two women were sympathetic because he had long opposed his party's entry into the government. Hildegart told him their adventure, at which Besteiro burst out laughing and advised her, as a young woman, to be more careful in the future. The time was not ripe for persuading backward people with radical slogans.

Hildegart was indignant. Pull back already, scarcely five months after the dictatorship had ended? When everything was in flux?

Party policy, said Besteiro. We cannot think only of the workers in the cities. Spain is a country without industry. With antiquated customs, it is true. But reeducation must proceed slowly. We mustn't offend people. Particularly the women. Our party was responsible for getting their right to vote through parliament. But we'll be the biggest loser in the next elections if we don't treat the women's question with the greatest restraint. Otherwise, it will be precisely the women who won't vote for us.

Realpolitik is irresponsible, Hildegart replied. It's spineless; it bites its own tail.

You're still so young, said Besteiro, angry now and ready to end the conversation. Why don't you step back from daily politics for a while and devote yourself to your studies, enjoy your youth, that sweet time, so long past for me!

A week later a delegation of Andalusian day laborers called on Hildegart to see if she would help them. They came from Jaén, and, against the advice of the leader of the anarcho-syndicalists, had voted Socialist. Now the *patrón* was taking revenge by not hiring them; he preferred to let the olives rot on the trees to hiring red workers. They had waited for the promised agrarian reform—a piece of land for everyone—but it never came, so they had come to the capital seeking help. At the ministry they had been sent from one desk to another. It seemed to them that they weren't welcome. They had wandered the corridors for a week without being allowed to present their case to the Socialist minister. Hildegart was their last hope.

The girl went to Luis Prieto, the minister's son and secretary, with a petition from the farm workers in her hand. Prieto took the paper, read it, and crumpled it.

Why are you doing that? Hildegart asked.

We get dozens of these every day.

That's no reason to throw them away. At least present their request to your father.

Why? Prieto asked. It doesn't matter whether I throw it away or the minister does it himself.

Before it became known that Hildegart had gone against party discipline, an editor of *El Socialista* printed an interview with her that appeared on the front page of the newspaper in December, 1931, four days before her seventeenth birthday. Against the will of her mother, who felt unwell and had taken to her bed, Hildegart went to the paper by herself. She had concluded her law studies in September and had immediately enrolled at the school of medicine, almost at the same time that three new books by her appeared, one of which, *The Sexual Rebellion of Youth*, didn't always reach the readers it was meant for. More than a few men of advanced years bought the book anticipating erotic subject matter. But, after skimming it, they put it on the shelf in disappointment, for rather than a depiction of inventive, shocking love, they found a passionate plea for the abolition of marriage, for a repeal of all laws antagonistic to women and children, and a support of birth-control measures. The journalist alluded to this work when he asked Hildegart what she considered the major problem of her time.

The sexual problem, the girl answered, is the key to all others. Large families, marital strife, violence, these are all a result of the same problem. The sexual revolution must come before all others. Spanish workers should not forget that.

What did Hildegart expect of the future?

Absolute equality between men and women. Most important, the economic liberation of women. Equal pay for equal work. Abolition of domestic labor. Only in this way would the subservience of women be eliminated, a subservience that drove them to prostitution and crime. Emancipation is impossible as long as women are not free to work.

At home Aurora Rodríguez, who cut out every article by and about her daughter, was the first to read the newspaper interview carefully. I believe that giving women the vote has damaged the liberal climate of the country. I am thinking of the fanatic women Catholics I met in the Basque provinces, of the women of the middle class and the aristocracy. And of a fact I have criticized so often in my writings, that at assemblies the workers speak out against the pernicious effects of religion, while at home their wives are decorating the house with the Sacred Heart of Jesus. For this reason, I believe that women's suffrage has done more harm than good.

Did you really say that?

The girl nodded. But naturally I added that women's right to vote represented progress despite all my misgivings.

Where does that appear?

Nowhere.

So your words were taken out of context, deliberately distorted, to sanctify a bad policy.

Hildegart said nothing.

I didn't raise you for that, Aurora said. To have you be so exploited.

You're right, said Hildegart. But what should I do?

Come to yourself again.

Again? Hildegart asked.

9

The worker is concerned only with his stomach—whether
it's full or empty. That is the entirety of his anarchism,
says a Socialist politician, in public, with no compunc-
tion. How unfortunate, wrote Hildegart, that he judges
others by his own standards. The stomach, whose grati-
fication such leaders are so concerned with, determines
their own politics. Ideals and convictions are insignificant. Insignificant also are heart and mind. Sexual revolution? Oh, that's only discussed at election meetings.
In refined language. Inequality and exploitation? An occasion to turn a clever phrase and garner applause, nothing more. And without thinking of their own homes or
work places, where these leaders treat their wives and
subordinates like dirt. Nationalization of the banks. Ex-
propriation of church property. State ownership of the
large estates. Also unimportant. Because they profit personally from these institutions. We have been silent, she
wrote, for too long.

The maid had already gone to bed when the telephone rang, long after midnight, as Hildegart sat at her typewriter. Aurora Rodríguez, who was keeping her company, stood and picked up the receiver.

You red whore. You and your immaculate daughter. You'll get it soon.

She hung up.

Who was it? Hildegart asked.

A wrong number.

Why are you lying?

I'm not lying, said Aurora Rodríguez. Or is there a Señor Sánchez living here?

No one dials a wrong number at this hour. Tell me the truth.

I'm not lying.

You are. Out of misplaced concern. As if we weren't strong enough, you and I, to deal with these attacks.

I often doubt that we are, said Aurora, hiding her head in her hands.

Hildegart was silent.

Go to bed, she said. I'll be finished soon.

Aurora stood up and went to the door. You're right. It was stupid of me. But it was a long time before she could sleep.

The next morning Aurora Rodríguez decided to buy a pistol from a fence, as it was impossible for a woman to get a gun license. In the maze of alleys surrounding the flea market, she purchased one from a gypsy, a barely used Luger, the man assured her, with fifty rounds of ammunition. He twice explained to her how to use it, then she went to pick up her daughter at the editorial offices of *La Tierra*, Guzmán's daily newspaper, where Hildegart was reviewing, in a series of articles, her four-year membership in the Socialist party. The girl, surrounded by the editors, was laughing, but fell silent as soon as she noticed Aurora.

Did you give them the manuscript? asked Aurora.

Hildegart nodded.

We'll print it tomorrow, Guzmán said.

Then we don't wish to disturb you any longer, said Aurora.

Not at all, the man said. It's a pleasure.

You must have a great deal to do. And Hildegart's work awaits her also.

But we don't have anything to do, Hildegart said as they left the building.

There is always work to be done, Aurora replied.

One day the British writer H. G. Wells arrived in Madrid from Irún. The newly-formed League for Sexual Reform, of which Hildegart was honorary secretary, had invited the Englishman to give a series of lectures. Because Hildegart was known to the English through several of her essays that had appeared in British journals, she was asked to take care of him during his visit and to serve as interpreter during his lectures, as he was not fluent in Spanish.

Following his first talk in the Ateneo, a long discussion developed between Wells and the girl, who rejected his line of reasoning on strict family planning. Finally, he fell back on Malthus, whose theory had been taken up by the propertied classes, afraid that the rapid reproduction rate of the workers and unpropertied peasants would threaten their privileges. Such a point of view was cynical, she said, not to mention outdated. It was not the rich who should profit from a drop in the birth rate, but those directly involved, women above all, who would no longer have their chances for work restricted, and the children, who, because they were fewer, would be more loved and encouraged and therefore would have a greater chance to develop themselves. And the working class as a whole, because it wouldn't have so much to consider in its struggles, would be harder to exploit, more adept, more united.

Wells tried to take the heart out of Hildegart's argument by stressing that he spoke in the name neither of a party nor of a movement, that his interest was of a general human nature. Emotions were of no help at all, objectivity was the thing. Of course there were emphatic differences between the conditions in his country and here, of which he had no direct knowledge, but that he wished to gain in Hildegart's experienced company. At any rate, all of humanity was in the same boat and changes here had their consequences there. He was amused by *the red virgin*. The vehemence with which she defended her position was a good sign, he said. People abroad had a romantic vision of this land, bullfights, flamenco, Mérimée; now he had discovered a new facet; how nice.

After they had eaten, the famous guest, who said he wanted to become acquainted with the distinctive life of Madrid, the world of the cloak-and-dagger plays, was taken to the Mesón del Segoviano in the center of the city. Wells, unused to the heady wine, rose after a while to seek the toilet. He returned quite pale.

My God, he said. I'm really drunk. I just saw elephants, lions, long-tailed monkeys.

Hildegart laughed. You're not hallucinating. That's the Borza Circus that winters in the courtyard.

Before Wells departed two weeks later, he asked to have a talk with Hildegart. He wished to thank her for the care that she had shown him during his stay, despite their differences of opinion. She had enormous talent. It would be irresponsibly twisted by the situation in Spain. He had a good friend, Havelock Ellis, somewhat a fool, to be sure, but an intelligent man, a sexologist. The girl could work with him; Wells need only say the word. She shouldn't worry about the details, money, a work permit, lodgings; he knew the Chancellor of the Exchequer personally.

Hildegart, overwhelmed by this offer, asked for a few weeks to think about it.

Take as much time as you wish, said Wells. I'll keep my word. A letter from you will do.

If it were up to me, you wouldn't need to wait. I've long dreamed of such an opportunity.

Of course, the man said. Your family. Your family will have something to say about it.

Politics, Hildegart replied. My friends would greatly miss me.

In September, 1932, the girl was expelled from the Youth Association because of behavior damaging to the party. Contrary to party by-laws, she was not served the decision; the commission also dispensed with summoning her to announce it. In October Hildegart published an extensive work that criticized socialism on two levels. On the one, she pointed out Marx's false prognosis, that the revolution would take place in the industrialized countries, France and Great Britain. On the other she depicted, in all the details of their machinations, the Spanish leaders, who, in her opinion, placed their own personal interests above those of the proletariat. In the afterword she commented on her resignation from all of the party organizations she had belonged to for four years.

A short time later she accepted an invitation to join the Federalist party, a party that played no great role nationally, as her mother stated in court, but that was led by men and women of integrity. Not a few of her friends were surprised by her decision; they had expected Hildegart to join the small but active group of Communists, particularly as the girl never tired of praising the sexual policies and new morality of the Soviet state and of expressing her hope to be permitted soon to travel to Russia. But Hildegart was of the opinion that each country must find its own way to socialism, and the way she saw the situation in Spain, where the population had a deep and justifiable distrust of centralized power, socialism would be arrived at only through the self-determination of the different peoples and regions.

Aurora Rodríguez later denied that she had influenced Hildegart's choice, but admitted that, at least in the beginning, she had been relieved.

The girl enjoyed the respect that her new comrades showed her, too much, in Aurora's estimation. After she met Abel Velilla, the only young man in the party leadership, at a meeting in Barcelona, there was a change in her, according to her mother. The girl, who had once confessed to Guzmán that she had not had a youth, lost the seriousness that she had exhibited up to then and showed an interest in things she had earlier thought little of. Aurora Rodríguez was surprised when her daughter suddenly wanted to pick out her own clothes. Hildegart also asked her mother for permission to wear necklaces, bracelets, and brooches when she went out. The maid tried to mediate the arguments that were provoked by this request. Aurora's anger turned then against Julia Sanz, and she, who had tried for the longest time without success to get the maid to address her as comrade, canceled her day off. When Hildegart found out about it, she accused her mother of undermining her own work. How could her essays and lectures remain credible when she preached water and drank wine? Aurora was ashamed.

She had hoped to become once again the center of Hildegart's life after her break with the Socialists. But the opposite occurred. She felt that she was increasingly being pushed aside. She was disturbed by Hildegart's frequent meetings with Velilla, though they took place in Aurora's presence, by her awakening vanity, and by her correspondence with Ellis and Magnus Hirschfeld* in English or German, languages that Aurora didn't understand. Strangers were taking possession of her daughter. What had brought about the change in Hildegart that threatened her so? It couldn't be herself; she had made no mistake she was aware of, except for the single unforgivable one that she never forgot, and that was the frivolity with which she had chosen that man, had allowed herself to be duped by him, Hildegart's father, no, her *physiological colleague,* as she called him in court. She wanted to know his fate, once and for all; what she knew about him haunted her like a nightmare.

*(Director, Institute of Sexology in Berlin)

She began cautiously to make inquiries, found out names and addresses of his relatives, used the occasion of a lecture by her daughter to the freethinkers of La Coruña to travel for a few hours to El Ferrol. She barely recognized the town of her childhood, and it took her longer than planned to find the house where the brother of the alleged priest lived. She rang the bell. Aurora gasped when the man opened the door; his resemblance to Hildegart's father was undeniable.

She asked, without introducing herself, what had become of his brother who had brought so much unhappiness upon his family, as she had found out years before.

The man stared at her. Dead.

Really? Really dead?

He hanged himself. Ten years ago.

Aurora Rodríguez thanked him for the information.

Wait, the man called after her. Who are you? But Aurora was gone.

The news comforted her, but did not erase her worry about Hildegart. The criminal was dead, she later said to Guzmán, but he had left traces behind. My daughter was in danger of giving in to the temptations of the flesh.

Hildegart gets prettier every day, announced one of Guzmán's editors. Soon we'll have to find a man for her!

Such coarse jokes are uncalled for, said Aurora. Besides, my daughter is already engaged.

Oh, I didn't know that. Please forgive me. And who is the fortunate young man?

Hildegart blushed and looked at her mother in astonishment.

A Norwegian biologist, Aurora Rodríguez said.

And when will they marry?

We will make that known in good time.

Hildegart looked at the floor. I know nothing about this, she said quietly.

And one last question: What do you think of love?

The way society is organized today, it is not worth it to love. Even in this area, capitalism and religion have set obstacles in the way of troublesome ideas. I'm for free love. And I believe that love is dependent on one's own will. For that reason, I have no intention of experiencing it until I am older and mature enough. One often mistakes a sudden mood or the sexual drive for love. And so this lovely and seemly word is dragged through the dirt, and our generation must first clean it off fastidiously before there can be a new morality under the sun.

10

Then Hildegart began to neglect her responsibilities. In the mornings she left the apartment to go to the newspaper's offices, as she told the maid, but she was seldom there, and she put off writing long-promised, overdue articles with the excuse of urgent duties owed the League for Sexual Reform. She returned home late in the evening, when only Aurora Rodríguez was still awake. She refused to tell her mother anything about her activities. When Aurora tried to get her to explain herself, she immediately went to her room and locked herself in, before her mother, reprimanding her in whispers, could stick her foot in the door. Unable to make anything of this behavior, Aurora Rodríguez paced her study and considered whether she had failed in her task.

When she arrived at breakfast one morning in a dejected mood, Julia Sanz told her that earlier, as she was going to the market, a black limousine had pulled up to her and a well-dressed older man had asked her from the back seat of the automobile if a certain Señorita Hildegart lived in this house, which the maid innocently affirmed.

Aurora Rodríguez was startled; she could not help judging this event as further evidence of devious attempts to remove Hildegart from her influence. The woman remembered several calls in the last weeks, when different male voices claimed to have dialed the repair shop of Hermanos Fuster. At the third disturbance of this sort, Aurora, certain that the calls were designed solely to break her will, screamed into the telephone that she would not be intimidated by such means. This is not a repair shop, and I will not hand over my daughter docilely, not at all, only over my dead body.

The next day a man appeared, a repairman who claimed that there was a disturbance in Aurora's telephone connection, a trick, the woman thought, to gain entry into the apartment and secretly plant a listening device, even though he acted totally unsuspiciously and the telephone company confirmed his visit when asked.

After Hildegart, as on the previous mornings, left the apartment quite early without explaining her conduct, Aurora Rodríguez went to her daughter's bedroom and removed the key from the door. When Hildegart returned late that evening, Aurora once again tried to engage her in conversation. The girl interrupted the attempt by saying that there was nothing more to discuss, and retired to her room, into which her mother, however, now followed.

Hildegart was furious that she could no longer lock her door and claimed that Aurora had no right to take such a step. She screamed, for the first time, it seemed to her mother: Go away, and leave me in peace!

In a soft voice, and alluding to the maid sleeping in the next room, Aurora pleaded with her not to make a scene. She could not understand her daughter's sudden change in behavior and suggested they have a talk and try to save what could be saved of their relationship.

Hildegart brusquely replied that Aurora had dominated her entire life, followed her for no reason, and guarded her to the extent that she could not believe her mother didn't know what was going on. She had decided, after Aurora Rodríguez had even chosen a husband for her without asking her opinion, to have her own way, to live freely and independently, just as she demanded in the writings that her mother had always approved.

At whose cost? Aurora asked.

I won't be a burden to you much longer, Hildegart replied. Not financially either, if that's what you mean.

She had accepted an offer from Wells and the sexologist Ellis; she had said nothing about the offer till now because she had long been uncertain about it. She would be leaving in the next few days, on the eleventh of June, the twelfth at the latest, and would continue her work in London under more favorable conditions.

At this news Aurora Rodríguez fainted, but quickly came to. At the moment she awoke, however, Hildegart said only that she was unmoved by Aurora's shock. Aurora, fighting her dizziness, responded that Hildegart had no right to take such a step. It was to her, her mother, that she owed her life and her positive, yes, ideal circumstances, her knowledge and her abilities. Hildegart had a mission that she had to realize, even at

the cost of self-sacrifice. Following Hildegart's disclosure, much that had been inconsistent of late was now
clear to her, she said. Dark forces had successfully in-
serted themselves between mother and daughter; they
wanted to force her to surrender through anonymous,
disturbing phone calls, and to flatter Hildegart with ex-
cessive praise.

You're dreaming. Who would want to turn us against
one another?

All of our enemies. The Socialist leaders want revenge, the priests, the monarchists. And Wells is a
screen for the British secret service.

Hildegart laughed. You've found an absurd reason for
something that needs no explanation. You alone are responsible for our necessary separation, with your presumptuous claims. I'm to exist only for others, for the
women, the proletariat, for humanity, and am supposed
to forget myself entirely.

So you want to go alone, Aurora asked, and leave me
here behind?

Naturally.

Then you are lost. Too weak to remain true to your
goals.

I'm strong, said Hildegart. I don't need you anymore.
But can the same be said of you?

That same night Aurora Rodríguez wrote an article in
which she presented her daughter's failure in the form
of a parable, as she later related to the High Court:

*Cain and Abel. We have been taught to hate Cain. He
has been represented as the first criminal of human history, as the first person to commit fratricide. In the tall
tales of the so-called holy scriptures, he is depicted in the
same way Wells later also depicted him: with a monkey's*

face, monkey's hands, crooked legs, and a receding forehead, abhorrent, that is, according to the tastes of today's
reader.

And yet Cain is the greatest hero of Christian mythol-
ogy. In order that the reader may comprehend the true
causes of Abel's death, I offer two quotes, one by Marc
Connelly, the other from George Bernard Shaw, two intelligent men of our time: "I was wukkin' in de fiel' an'
he was sittin' in de shade of de tree." "He laughed at me;
and then came my great idea; why not kill him as he
killed the beasts? I struck; and he died, just as they did.
Then I gave up your old silly drudging ways, and lived
as he had lived, by the chase, by the killing, and by the
fire. Am I not better than you? stronger, happier, freer?"

Who then is Abel? If we bear these quotes in mind,
then we see in him the forerunner of the Socialist politicians who laugh at the workers, who are lazy, who reject
everything that is averse to their comfort. A propagandist
of sloth, who wants neither to learn nor to fight, and who
avoids honest competition.

Cain, on the other hand, is the symbol of progress. He
is the first anarchist. And, as such, he is rebellious. He
does not belong to those who are content and satiated.
He is a genius. Abel would never have emerged from the
anonymous masses had not the Bible depicted him as a
victim, as if the fact that he was one was not already
proof of his inferiority. As for the rest, he is surrounded
by the aura of the pious, foolish little convent student. He
is the enemy of progress, far from the tumultuous path of
civilization, incapable of fighting and of loving. A small
spirit; Cain, in contrast, is great.

So it is necessary to emulate Cain, who cleared all
obstacles from his path, even his brother, an act of puri-

fication. Cain is already human. Abel is still a puppet in God's hands. What does the Bible offer that is more beautiful than Cain, who defied God's will and destroyed a life that was no life, because it had no will!

Cain is the symbol of resistance against everything traditional. Abel, the symbol of mediocrity. Cain is the shepherd, Abel a sheep of the herd. How fortunate a society in which there were only people like Cain! Though that is probably impossible. To recognize them, it is necessary to have others, the flock of Abels, the stupid ones who laugh at us.

The one who dies is always considered the victim, never the one whose act, as regrettable as it may be, is inherently great. Whoever, like Abel, conforms to the old order, whoever gives in, stops halfway to his goal, has forfeited his life. Cain had a responsibility to kill Abel. He could not do otherwise. The victim provoked the crime.

Hildegart agreed with the article. Though I know what you want to say to me with it. That I am Abel, lazy and self-satisfied. But that is not true. I want to be free, not to be subordinate to another's will. To live like Cain.

If you leave me, Aurora said, all is lost.

Hildegart shrugged her shoulders. Then you are the weaker.

Aurora Rodríguez gave up. Later, when Hildegart and the maid had left the apartment, she took the pistol and climbed the stairs to the attic, where she called to memory the fence's instructions and loaded the gun. Then she raised her arm and put the barrel to her temple. She must have stood like that for a long time, motionless; when she came to herself, it was already twilight.

In the kitchen, Julia Sanz told her that Señorita Hildegart had let her know that in the next few days she would be departing on a trip for an unspecified period of time. She had told her to have two suitcases taken to the train station for her.

That is correct, Aurora Rodríguez said. We will leave in a week. For Mallorca. The ocean air will do Hildegart good. We shall return in a month. In the interim, you will take care of the household. You can also go to visit your relatives for a few days. But do not let anyone into the apartment, not even your best friends.

Madam can rest assured. But what about the dogs? I can't take them with me.

Take them to our neighbor. She's good with dogs.

Hildegart returned in the evening.

Where were you? Aurora asked.

At the editorial offices. To say goodbye. I also took them your article.

Without asking my permission?

Why? After all, Hildegart taunted her, we are one heart and one soul. Anyway, it will appear under my name. Because it could just as well have been written by me.

We are going to Mallorca, said Aurora.

You are going to Mallorca. My decision stands.

Aurora once again began to castigate her. Ignoring the maid's presence, she accused Hildegart of betraying her, of mental prostitution, similar to the physical, only more abominable.

For two days and two nights, during which she forced her daughter to go without sleep, Aurora Rodríguez tried in vain to bring about her change of heart. On the eighth of June, on the morning of a hot, early summer's day, Hildegart, with an empty, expressionless face, once again left the house. She returned later that same morning. Mother and daughter locked themselves into the study. Earlier, Aurora had told the maid they were not to be disturbed. Meals were canceled. They had to discuss the details of their trip to the Mediterranean.

In court, Aurora Rodríguez stated that, in view of her daughter's obstinacy, she had considered resorting to her final means and revealing to Hildegart her father's character. But this disclosure proved unnecessary. Something must have transpired during the short time Hildegart was away, a meeting, a phone call, perhaps she received a letter, something that made clear to her that Aurora's fears were justified. Hildegart was shaken and insecure on her return. She, Aurora, had taken advantage of this condition and had again and again, rapidly and bitterly, repeated her opinion that Hildegart's decision to leave her mother was nothing more than the betrayal of her ideals and her capitulation before the enemy.

By nightfall her arguments began to take effect. Hildegart cried, for the first time in four years. She told Aurora she was right, but confessed that she was too weak, too exhausted, too burned out, to fulfill the mission that her mother had destined her for. She lacked the strength for the battle and above all for the victory. She felt there was an abyss between herself and her goal; she just wanted to sleep, for weeks, for years, to play, to rest. She had recognized much too late that the whole world wanted only to remove her from her mother's protection. Now she was aware of it, Aurora had convinced her, but she feared, no, knew, that on the next day she would feel different, would again succumb to the temptation to be led from the straight and narrow. Then she fell silent, sobbing, and finally, in a tone that she, Aurora, would never be able to forget, cried: Help me, Mother, please help me!

When Aurora asked how she could help, Hildegart answered that, because she saw no way out, she had thought of suicide, but was too cowardly to go through with it. She, Aurora, had created Hildegart; it was up to her now to sacrifice her work that had failed. If she did not do so, she quickly added when she saw Aurora's panic, her mother would deeply regret it the next day. Aurora Rodríguez gave in to her request after long, admittedly half-hearted resistance, for she knew that Hildegart was right.

Before she went to bed, the maid heard whispering in the study. As Aurora Rodríguez had forbidden her to enter the room, she bent down to the keyhole and saw Hildegart sitting on her mother's lap, something that had never been allowed before. The girl had one arm around the other woman's neck, a cheek pressed to her shoulder, her eyes closed, and said over and over again: You will do it. Isn't that right? Promise me.

Yes, Aurora said, I'll do it tonight. But sleep now.

When, two hours later, she heard by Hildegart's quiet, even breathing that she had fallen into a deep sleep, she carried her daughter, not without effort, into her room, laid her down carefully on the bed, and threw a blanket over her. Then she pulled up a chair, sat down and *surrendered myself to my pain.*

Hildegart slept quietly.

In the morning around eight, Aurora heard the maid leaving the apartment. A little later she stood up and got the pistol from her bedroom.

11

On June 9, 1933, around noon, the anarcho-syndi-
calist, Eduardo de Guzmán, editor-in-chief of the daily
newspaper *La Tierra*, set out for the forensic institute of
the city of Madrid, after hearing the startling, horrible
news. In front of the building, on the street that widened
into a plaza, stood several groups of women, well-
dressed and wearing makeup, as he noted with disap-
proval, who were busy discussing what had happened.
It was not shock he observed, but that not unpleasant
shudder of excitement those members of the upper class
exhibit at the sorrow of those different from themselves.
In spite of this, it surprised him that their faces lacked
the proper solemnity, pain, sorrow.

Guzmán, having identified himself as a journalist and
friend of the deceased, entered the morgue situated
above the inner courtyard. He was received there by Dr.
Alberich, one of the doctors who had performed the au-
topsy and who led him past body parts and blood-
soaked cloths to a stone table on which Hildegart lay,

naked except for a cardboard tag on her foot. The first bullet, he said, penetrated her heart, killing her instantaneously. To all appearances the act occurred while the victim was asleep. Due to the onset of decomposition, the corpse had received several injections of formaldehyde and glycerin.

Hildegart's body appeared intact, despite her wounds. Her dark, wavy hair concealed the bullet holes and the burn traces caused by the pistol's being placed so close to her skin. Her eyes were closed and her mouth slightly open, as if to smile. He looked at her full but waxy cheeks, the short, somewhat stocky neck. It confused the young man to see the girl, who had for the last three years been the most intense, but always unapproachable colleague of his newspaper, undressed, her heavy breasts sloping outward, her thick pubic hair. While she was alive, Hildegart had the ability to make a man forget sensual desire. Guzmán turned away.

In front of the building he met a group of women from the textile factory in Carabanchel. They were taking their lunchtime to pay Hildegart their respects, with red carnations that they now held on to, as the doorman would not allow them to enter the building. Only a few months before, the now-deceased had talked with them, had been the only political figure they addressed who was prepared to support them in their struggle.

But what, they asked the journalist, about the rumors flying around everywhere? That Aurora, her own mother, with whom she was of one heart and one soul, had committed the deed. Tell us that isn't so. That it was someone else. Bandits. Please! *Today, four pistol shots fired in the early-morning hours destroyed a girl in*

*the prime of her life, and extinguished the hope embodied
by this extraordinary representative of Spanish youth.
What led to this tragic event, which all of Spain is moved
by? We have asked ourselves this question again and
again since the first, still vague rumors were confirmed.
Hildegart was killed by her own mother, the mother who
had always been at her side, selfless and generous, whose
only concern was her daughter. There was never any mis-
trust or quarrel between them, not even the minor annoy-
ances unavoidable in family life. As is known, Aurora's
interrogation has begun; it is not presumptuous to assume that, in her excess of love for her daughter, she
could not accept that Hildegart wished to separate from
her. Aurora Rodríguez could have committed this crime
only in a state of temporary insanity.* Guzmán's colleagues in the editorial offices of more conservative papers were at no less a loss. But they, whose scorn
Hildegart had not been spared during her lifetime, used
this opportunity to call attention to the evil consequences of militant feminism. Something like this is to
be expected when women, who are by nature unsuited
to intellectual endeavors, assume radical positions. Her
hatred of all men turned Aurora Rodríguez into the murderer of her own child. Or: Hildegart herself had allegedly long practiced the sexual freedom that she never
tired of propagating. Otherwise well-informed circles
did not consider it to be out of the question that Hildegart had bled to death during an improper abortion. Or
that she was killed by her mother when she revealed
to her that she was pregnant. The rumor also circu-
lated that Aurora Rodríguez was not Hildegart's natural
mother at all, a conjecture that Guzmán had already

heard at the forensic institute. Taboo, lesbian love was mentioned, love that had ended in blood when the younger woman resisted.

On the second day all of these accounts proved untenable. The papers now quoted alleged friends of the two women who maintained that they had witnessed a quarrel between Hildegart and her mother. Hildegart's decision to leave her mother was, in their opinion, to be traced back to her succumbing to the courtship of her party comrade, the Deputy Mayor of Barcelona, Abel Velilla. Velilla had asked Aurora Rodríguez for her daughter's hand, but had been refused. Hildegart, as Aurora supposedly said to the man, is not on this earth to be married. She is here to fulfill her mission. Your feelings for one another will not endure. Then Hildegart cried and gave in to her wishes. But Aurora Rodríguez must have believed that this submission would not last.

Don Abel Velilla, an attorney in Barcelona, was soon heard from. At first in a telegram to *La Tierra*, whose political views conformed to his own. In his dispatch, he urged a disclaimer of the sensationalistic version of the motivation for the crime, which was disrespectful and degrading to the distinguished deceased, as well as to himself. I never spoke to Hildegart about what is now alleged to be a love relationship, nor did I ask for her hand in marriage, or even visit her at her residence. I never harbored any feelings for her other than admiration for her enormous talent and gratitude for her selfless cooperation, the loss of which the Federalist party will not recover from for a long while. In addition, he explained in a long-distance call to another newspaper, I long ago directed my personal feelings elsewhere.

The funeral took place on the eleventh of June, attended by tens of thousands, though it was a weekday. The funeral procession, which ended in the suburb of Las Ventas, was joined by many members of parliament, trade unionists, and prominent intellectuals, but was largely made up of simple workingwomen, as Guzmán noted. Hildegart was buried in the Civil Cemetery, in unconsecrated earth, set aside for the godless.

In the prison at Noviciado, Aurora Rodríguez was assigned a single cell. She was considered rebellious by the officials. She sharply criticized the facilities, the daily routine, and the food, all of which criticism the guards found unjustified. She demanded to be put with the other prisoners. Her request was turned down by the warden. She then managed to be allowed to take part in the daily rounds in the courtyard. She planted herself in the middle of the quad and gathered the other women around her. She demanded changes be made in the penal system: An extension of visitation rights. An increase in the amount of mail inmates could receive. A fair wage for work performed by prisoners. Fresh fruit and vegetables at every meal. The establishment of a prison library. But we can't read, the women said. Literacy! Aurora cried. Decent underwear, the prisoners replied. Books, Aurora screamed. Meat and makeup, the others chanted. Then the guards forced Aurora back.

She did not appear to be discouraged by this lack of success. She asked for paper and a typewriter, and drew up an outline for prison reform. More respect, she demanded, deference! Be glad that I am among you; my proposals will be to your advantage; you will lead a more honorable life.

The inmates called her "the crazy one," wove her a crown of reeds, draped a dirty towel on her, and led her around the courtyard. She did not defend herself.

The attorney Mariano López, who had taken on the case when his predecessor was appointed to the ministry, was pleased when he heard complaints concerning Aurora's strange behavior. She knows what she's doing. I shall base my defense on my client's being of unsound mind.

Aurora Rodríguez didn't understand. I take total responsibility for my act. I committed it after full consideration. It wasn't easy for me. I'm supposed to be suffering delusions? Because I support the reeducation of prostitutes? Because I am of the opinion that the gypsies should organize? That women should have the same rights as men?

These remarks have nothing in the least to do with the trial, said the presiding judge. The defendant will refrain from such statements and address the case.

The trial took place less than a year after Hildegart's death. Hours before the proceedings began, the area around the Palace of Justice presented an unusual picture. The first of the crowd of curious onlookers had arrived the evening before. They passed the time until they could be admitted with music and dance. Beggars took advantage of the situation, jugglers, vendors of refreshments and sweets. To the amusement of the men around them, two women standing in line next to each other began to fight, tore each other's hair, fell to the ground clawing one another. A policeman used strong blows to separate them.

Those attending were searched for weapons. The court received anonymous death threats; an assassination was feared. In the months since Hildegart's death the number of children murdered had doubled. Women who up until then had been unobtrusive, irreproachable, killed their daughters, still others named their newborns Hildegart, young men used the name to make fun of their fiancées if they interested themselves in politics or the women's question, or sometimes only if they read the newspaper or picked up a book. That's not for a woman. If you continue like this, you'll end up like Hildegart.

At the beginning of the trial Aurora Rodríguez was quiet and contained. She held in her hand a red carnation that a woman had given her as two female guards led her into the courtroom. She answered the prosecutor's questions in a loud, clear voice. When she mentioned political events, the presiding judge interrupted her and forbade her incendiary comments. If it happened again, he threatened, the trial would take place behind closed doors. If that is the case, said Aurora, I will refrain from further comments.

On the first day of the proceedings, two experts appointed by the court, the conservative doctors Vallejo Nájera and Piga, read their findings: Aurora Rodríguez Carballeira is a psychopath. She suffers from exhibitionism and a persecution complex. She exhibits strong feelings of hate. Her natural mother instinct is aberrant. But she was mentally competent when she committed the murder. She is paranoid, but not psychotic, therefore she is fully responsible for her act.

The next morning their statements were contradicted by the psychiatrists appointed by the defense. The doctors Sacristán, Prado, and Fuertes had examined Aurora

Rodríguez immediately following her crime and in the
weeks thereafter, often and thoroughly. All of their tests
and examinations confirmed their first suspicion that the
accused suffered from incurable paranoia. For this reason she could not be held responsible for the offense of
which she was accused.

Following this opinion, the experts broke out in ve-
hement argument. Each accused the other of incompetence, egotism, and irresponsibility. The prosecutor
asked Aurora Rodríguez if she considered herself to be
mentally ill. For the first time, the woman lost her composure, sprang up and grasped the railing in front of her
so strongly that her knuckles turned white.

No, and no again!

There you have it, the man said; no other evidence is
necessary.

Objection! cried the defense.

You strike out at me to attack reforms, Aurora
screamed. You're not against me, you're against progress.

The judge silenced her. I will not allow this woman
to make a political martyr of herself. The hearings were
postponed to subdue emotions.

*Nervousness—that, in a word, is the mood here in the
courtroom. The women at the hearing are nervous and
follow the trial in great agitation. Most are convinced
that the accused is guilty. But many are not afraid to
declare their sympathy for Aurora Rodríguez; they even
exhibit understanding, if one lends credence to their
whispered comments. The experts are nervous, the prosecutor is nervous, the counsel for the defense. The accused,
unlike yesterday, is also nervous, and nervous above all,*

to an unbelievable degree, are the witnesses. Those who
had gotten to know Aurora Rodríguez through Hildegart's political work, among them ministers, municipal
councilors, and university professors, were excused
from appearing as witnesses. Those who were left were
the maid, Julia Sanz, the porter's wife in Aurora's building, numerous women neighbors, and several men who
maintained they had a close, exclusively paternal relationship with the deceased. Aurora Rodríguez vigor-
ously repudiated their statements. When the maid,
intimidated by the many people in the room, began to
stutter and gasped out that Aurora had often struck her
daughter, Hildegart's mother interrupted her. You lie,
Julia. And you know it very well. There was a disturbance when the counsel for the defense announced that
Hildegart's father was in the courtroom. Aurora denied
it, swearing that the man had been dead for years.

Then the prosecutor began his summing-up. He
stressed that he personally rejected a trial by jury, *one
of the many negative achievements of democracy*, but that
he nevertheless welcomed the fact that the jury was
made up solely of men, who, as opposed to women,
were not led by their feelings and were open to rational
arguments. The defendant, *highly perverse*, committed
the crime for three reasons: because her daughter
wished to lead an independent life; because Hildegart
had fallen in love; because Hildegart had turned her
back to politics. Aurora Rodríguez's crime was premed-
itated and was not committed as an act of passion. She
was, in addition, a woman of average intelligence. The
accused is clever, nothing more. Mediocre. He reproached the defense for not being interested in the

truth, but concerned only with convincing the court of the accused's mental incompetence.

On the third and last day of the trial, Aurora's lawyer presented his case. He referred to the fact that there were several cases of insanity in her family, that her sex life, as proved by her past, was stunted, that the psychiatrists appointed by him had submitted their affidavit without remuneration, while the gentlemen Vallejo Nájera and Piga had charged extravagantly for theirs, that one of them had set eyes on Aurora Rodríguez for the first time in the courtroom. Not to mention the fact that they viewed Hildegart's work for the League of Sexual Reform with scorn and dismissal.

The accused is incurably ill; she must not be held accountable for her actions; I plead for her committal to a private institution.

The judge asked Aurora Rodríguez if she wished to add anything to these remarks.

Yes, Your Honor. I am in agreement with not one of defense's points. I am not crazy.

At one o'clock the verdict was announced. Aurora Rodríguez was found guilty of having killed her daughter Hildegart with shots fired from a pistol. The accused was of sound mind at the time she committed the crime. There were no mitigating circumstances.

Aurora Rodríguez was sentenced to incarceration for a period of twenty-six years, eight months and one day, with an additional punishment of a day of fasting every three months. The charge of possession of an unregistered weapon was dropped on the next day, as this offense fell under an amnesty decree declared by the government.

A year and a half later, Aurora was sent to a mental home following another psychiatric examination. The case did not come to appeal, for several months later four generals led a revolt against the government. In the confusion of civil war, Guzmán wrote, all traces of Aurora were lost.

12

Ciempozuelos, a village in the Jarama Valley, three hundred meters above sea level, lay for several weeks in the no-man's land between the fronts. Its population piled their possessions on carts and fled thirty-five kilometers to the capital at the approach of Franco's troops. Left behind were the frightened inmates of two mental institutions (one for men, one for women), shrapnel and mortars whistling over their heads. At the outbreak of war, most of the staff of the women's institution had fled to relatives in the hinterland. A few nuns refused to abandon the patients. But they were clearly of no help to them; at the sound of battle they locked themselves in the chapel and prayed for victory by the putschists, who had been appointed by God.

At the beginning of her stay in Ciempozuelos Aurora Rodríguez had proposed reforms of institutional life. She demanded two months' annual vacation for the nurses, for example. Curable patients should be dismissed at once and receive ambulatory treatment if they so wished. For the incurable, she demanded the establishment of autonomous communes. The doctors would be permitted to perform marriages only in exceptional cases. The choice of companions would be left up to the patients.

When the patients were left to themselves, following the flight and confusion of the nursing staff, Aurora appointed herself responsible for their well-being. Under her leadership the women blew up the main gate and settled in the houses of the village. A week later they had exhausted the provisions that had been left behind and they began to grow their own food. They quickly accustomed themselves to the presence of the war. They barely missed their medical care.

In February of 1937, a battalion of the national army occupied the village. The women were driven back into the hospital. Twenty days later General Franco, on his way to Palencia, inspected Ciempozuelos; with him came new doctors. The psychiatric hospitals were put under military sovereignty.

Aurora Rodríguez, who as ringleader spent several months in solitary, became depressed and discouraged at the outset of the Franco regime. She stopped reading newspapers and refused to work. She swallowed her food listlessly. Only one of the doctors, Juan Martínez, succeeded in breaking her silence. He nodded when she spoke of the necessity of radically restricting the birth rate. But then she found out that he had just become a father for the fourth time. Thereafter she avoided him. How is humanity to survive if everyone breeds like rabbits? Sometimes she still conversed with Dr. Alberdi. Until she heard that he took communion every Sunday. Priest's pawn. She turned all of her attention to a cat, and long mourned its death. She lived on, never speaking. She is reported to have died on the twenty-eighth of December, 1955.

13

Twenty years after the trial, after he had published an article in Hildegart's memory, Eduardo de Guzmán received a letter from Barcelona.

Dear friend!

I read with interest and approval your article which honors the life and influence of my daughter Hildegart. I am in agreement with everything you wrote about her. I would, however, add one, insignificant detail: you are of the opinion that Hildegart's mother, whom you lost contact with after her trial, died years ago. That is an error. I am alive and well.

In highest esteem!
Aurora Rodríguez Carballeira

Guzmán, who had not been informed of Aurora's transfer to Ciempozuelos, went in search of the return address on the envelope. But he found no one there. Nor could the neighbors tell him anything about the origin of the letter. Having failed to achieve his goal, he returned home.

AFTERWORD

In retrospect, the author finds it difficult to order and disentangle the accumulation of facts and implications. Propriety dictates, however, naming at least the most important documents, without which the story offered here could not have been told: Hildegart's articles that appeared between May, 1929, and June, 1933, in the daily press (above all in *El Socialista* and *La Tierra*); her books and booklets, thirteen in all; the substance of the conversations that Eduardo de Guzmán held with Aurora Rodríguez in prison following the crime, which he quoted in his book, *Mi hija Hildegart* (1977); as well as the court reports that appeared in the Madrid newspapers *El Sol*, *Heraldo de Madrid*, and *La Tierra* in May, 1934.

This account was supported by a grant from the Magistrate of the City of Vienna. With many thanks.

Erich Hackl was born in Steyr, Austria, in 1954, and studied German literature at the University of Vienna. After a career as lecturer first at the University of Madrid, then at the University of Vienna, he became a full-time writer, journalist, and critic. He received a grant to write this book from the town of Vienna, where he lives with his family.

VINTAGE INTERNATIONAL

VINTAGE INTERNATIONAL

___ Spring Snow by Yukio Mishima	$10.95	679-72241-6
___ Runaway Horses by Yukio Mishima	$10.95	679-72240-8
___ The Temple of Dawn by Yukio Mishima	$10.95	679-72242-4
___ The Decay of the Angel by Yukio Mishima	$10.95	679-72243-2
___ Cities of Salt by Abdelrahman Munif	$12.95	394-75526-X
___ Ada, or Ardor by Vladimir Nabokov	$10.95	679-72522-9
___ Bend Sinister by Vladimir Nabokov	$8.95	679-72727-2
___ The Defense by Valdimir Nabokov	$8.95	679-72722-1
___ Despair by Vladimir Nabokov	$7.95	679-72343-9
___ Invitation to a Beheading by Vladimir Nabokov	$7.95	679-72531-8
___ King, Queen, Knave by Vladimir Nabokov	$8.95	679-72340-4
___ Laughter in the Dark by Vladimir Nabokov	$8.95	679-72450-8
___ Lolita by Vladimir Nabokov	$7.95	679-72316-1
___ Look at the Harlequins! by Vladimir Nabokov	$8.95	679-72728-0
___ Mary by Vladimir Nabokov	$6.95	679-72620-9
___ Pale Fire by Vladimir Nabokov	$8.95	679-72342-0
___ Pnin by Vladimir Nabokov	$7.95	679-72341-2
___ Speak, Memory by Vladimir Nabokov	$9.95	679-72339-0
___ Strong Opinions by Vladimir Nabokov	$8.95	679-72609-8
___ Transparent Things by Vladimir Nabokov	$6.95	679-72541-5
___ A Bend in the River by V. S. Naipaul	$7.95	679-72202-5
___ A Turn in the South by V. S. Naipaul	$8.95	679-72488-5
___ Black Box by Amos Oz	$8.95	679-72185-1
___ The Shawl by Cynthia Ozick	$6.95	679-72926-7
Dictionary of the Khazars by Milorad Pavić		
___ male edition	$9.95	679-72461-3
___ female edition	$9.95	679-72754-X
___ Swann's Way by Marcel Proust	$9.95	679-72009-X
___ Grey Is the Color of Hope		
by Irina Ratushinskaya	$8.95	679-72447-8
___ Selected Poetry by Rainer Maria Rilke	$10.95	679-72201-7
___ Shame by Salman Rushdie	$9.95	679-72204-1
___ No Exit and 3 Other Plays by Jean-Paul Sartre	$7.95	679-72516-4
___ And Quiet Flows the Don by Mikhail Sholokhov	$10.95	679-72521-0
___ Ake: The Years of Childhood by Wole Soyinka	$9.95	679-72540-7
___ Confessions of Zeno by Italo Svevo	$9.95	679-72234-2
___ On the Golden Porch by Tatyana Tolstaya	$8.95	679-72843-0
___ The Optimist's Daughter by Eudora Welty	$8.95	679-72883-X
___ Losing Battles by Eudora Welty	$8.95	679-72882-1
___ The Eye of the Story by Eudora Welty	$8.95	679-73004-4
___ The Passion by Jeanette Winterson	$7.95	679-72437-0

Now at your bookstore or call toll-free to order: 1-800-733-3000
(credit cards only).